# THE SECOND
# COMING

## SHUBHA MENON

HarperCollins *Publishers* India

First published in India in 2014 by
HarperCollins *Publishers* India

Copyright © Shubha Menon 2014

P-ISBN: 978-93-5136-370-5
E-ISBN: 978-93-5136-371-2

2 4 6 8 10 9 7 5 3 1

Shubha Menon asserts the moral right
to be identified as the author of this work.

This is a work of fiction and all characters and incidents described
in this book are the products of the author's imagination. Any
resemblance to actual persons, living or dead, is entirely coincidental.

**HarperCollins *Publishers***
A-75, Sector 57, Noida, Uttar Pradesh 201301, India
77-85 Fulham Palace Road, London W6 8JB, United Kingdom
Hazelton Lanes, 55 Avenue Road, Suite 2900, Toronto, Ontario M5R
3L2 and 1995 Markham Road, Scarborough, Ontario M1B 5M8, Canada
25 Ryde Road, Pymble, Sydney, NSW 2073, Australia
10 East 53rd Street, New York NY 10022, USA

Typeset in 11/14 Dante MT by
R. Ajith Kumar

Printed and bound at
Thomson Press (India) Ltd

*For all my friends who have tried matrimony*
*and been tried by it.*

# THE SECOND COMING

Shubha Menon is a copywriter with a leading advertising agency. A practising Buddhist, she dreams of living in the hills where she can read, write and grow climbing roses. She lives in Delhi with her husband, daughter and two Dachshunds. This is her first book.

# 1

*She stood shivering in the balcony, her translucent, red negligeé aflutter in the breeze. Would he come as promised and rescue her from her dreary existence? Working quickly, she tied the rope to the balustrade and threw the other end down below. Behind her, the house was silent as a church. As she gazed fearfully into the distance, a faint glimmer of light appeared. It was a beacon in the dark for the pale damsel.*

*He was astride a black motorbike, his face hidden by a jet-black helmet. Behind him, his satin cloak billowed like a sail. The headlights glowed like burning embers, fanning the flames of her passion. A shiver ran down her spine. Was it fear or anticipation? There was no time to reflect upon the question. She knew she had to act quickly. Clutching the rope with delicate fingers, she leapt forward, and took the plunge, falling straight into the arms of her fair knight on his black charger. He gave her a shouldering look, revving the engine and they thundered away into the mysterious night...*

The motorbike's engine exploded right in Mini's ear, forcing her to look up from the book. It was Shyam, asleep on the next bed, emitting a volley of rumbling, ear-splitting snores.

Mini shook him. 'Shyam! *Stop snoring!*' He turned over, jiggly belly upwards, legs askew, nonchalantly switching to a softer, whistle-like rendition.

Mini sighed. She could kill him, this fat slob to whom she was married. Not an iota of romance in his oversized body, and – as though that weren't enough – he had to disturb her just when she had almost reached the steamy part of the book.

It had been fifteen years since she'd married Shyam. The excitement of the early days had waned far too quickly, leaving in its wake a dismal familiarity. Mini longed for a touch of romance but life had taught her that romance in a marriage was an oxymoron. Still, Mini hadn't given up. One of these days, she told herself, her knight in shining armour, her Dream Lover – DL for short – would arrive, sweep her off her feet and make passionate, romantic, fervent love to her.

Mini sighed. In the meantime, the best thing, to go to bed with, was a good book.

If books were Mini's first love, food was a close second. She checked to see that Shyam was in a  deep slumber before sneaking a plump hand under the mattress, where she had hidden a bar of Diet Swiss Ultra Creamy Delight. As always, chocolate filled her with a sense of absolute well-being. Better than sex, Mini decided, especially if you weren't getting any, and Mini hadn't seen action for a while now. Shyam would rather romance his laptop or his car. He actually called his car 'Sweetie'. Yechhhh! Not that she cared. Soon, very soon, Dream Lover would arrive to rescue her from her dreary existence. That would teach Sicko Shyam, thought Mini, as she turned her back to him and fell asleep.

When she woke up the next morning, Shyam had already left for the day, without bothering to bid her goodbye. Mini glanced at the clock and galvanized into action. She had to be in office in an hour. Flitting in and out of the shower in record time, she pulled on the first kurta she could lay her hands on. It tore with a hissing sound. Damn. She pulled on another one. A button popped and rolled off under the bed. Murphy's Law at work, Mini figured. When you have an early appointment, the universe will conspire to make you super late. She looked frantically for the extra-extra-large salwar-kameez she had bought earlier in the month and yanked it on, thankful that it still fit. The relief was short-lived. The mirror sounded an alarm; Mini stared at herself in disbelief. Gosh! She looked like an inflatable balloon. She was *fat*. No wonder there was no Mills & Boon hero in her life, she despaired. Which man would lay his life down for a blimp? How romantic could a man get with a double chin? That too, one with a tiny, black hair sprouting from it? This had to stop. Determination writ large on her face, she marched into the kitchen, opened the fridge and made herself a healthy, low-calorie salad using extra-virgin olive oil for dressing. There, that was all she was going to eat for lunch. On the refrigerator door, she stuck a paper on which she scribbled her diet for the week.

Breakfast – skimmed milk, one cup.

Lunch – salad.

Evening – green tea with dry toast.

Dinner – fruits.

Now all she had to do was follow the diet plan and she would be a size zero in no time. Feeling more in control, she stomped out of the house, laptop swinging dangerously from one arm and a tiffin box from the other.

The car started with a smooth purr and Mini stepped on the accelerator, ignoring the red light at the signal. The traffic policeman darted out from behind a tree and took down her car number. Behind her, a pretty young thing jumped the red light too and the man let her go with a smile. Life was so unfair, Mini thought bitterly. Just because she was fat, didn't mean she had to be challaned for it. Soon, she promised herself, she would reduce to a size zero and then life would move into fourth gear.

In a huff, Mini got out of the car in the basement parking and trudged moodily to the lift. 'Which floor, auntyji?' the lift boy piped up. Mini looked behind her to see who he was addressing. She was the only woman in the elevator. Feeling wretched, she entered Soul Mates, the place where she had been working for the last five years.

Soul Mates planned dream weddings. Mini loved her work. The sheer romance of the job was what she adored. Setting up the perfect venue, dreaming up an innovative theme, packing the bride's trousseau, the decor, the invitations ... Mini got a real rush out of it. At least somebody's romantic fantasies were coming alive. Mini basked vicariously in the joy of the newly-weds. Let the poor young things enjoy their moment before the inevitable disillusions set in, Mini figured.

She waved out to her friend and colleague, Deepa. They were close and shared lunch every day, along with gossip and news. Both of them worked in the creative section of the agency. The founder-owner of Soul Mates was the harried Mr Mahatta. Mini, the oldest and the most experienced employee, was his right hand. It was a small, homely little outfit, modest and personal, having only recently opened their new office in Mumbai.

Soul Mates had a reputation for uniqueness and creativity, the credit for which went largely to Mini. She brought the same passion to each wedding, irrespective of the size and scale. Mahatta being the typical Delhi businessman, had contacts everywhere. Mini had planned weddings for politicians, lottery kings and booze barons. But her most memorable experience, so far, had been the wedding of a businessman who was a secret nudist. In spite of the many hilarious moments the wedding had afforded her, she still remembered how she had wept when the couple had taken their vows. Marriage was such a joke, she reflected, but weddings could be sublime.

This week, they were working on the wedding of a young, page-three regular. Madam was fussy and had already rejected some brilliant themes suggested by the Soul Mates team. Now, Mahatta wanted Mini to take over and push an idea down the spoilt brat's throat. The meeting was scheduled for that day. Mini was prepared. She quickly checked her presentation and headed for the conference room. Just as she had connected her laptop to the projector, Mahatta walked in with the bride-to-be.

Mini gave her the once-over. Purple jeans, sneakers, short hair with streaks of pink, a tattoo below her ear. This one wouldn't settle for a regular wedding; she would go in for something bizarre.

Mini began the presentation. Her idea was to put the bride and groom in a hot-air balloon with a pundit, and have them take their wedding vows in the sky. Flying above the balloon, a helicopter would shower flowers and blessings. The relatives would watch the proceedings on giant screens below, while waiters circulated with champagne and balloon-shaped snacks. And, if it could be arranged, the couple could travel to their honeymoon in their balloon, floating down dreamily to the chosen destination. Mini moved from slide to slide, spinning out a magical evening. The socialite was sold. She wanted Mini to help her decide what kind of wedding dress would work best in a hot-air balloon. Mini gave it serious thought and suggested gold-and-pink harem pants, the kind that ballooned up when filled with air. Delighted, the socialite walked away, blowing kisses all around, causing Mahatta to blush.

At lunchtime, Deepa waved Mini over to her desk. Leaning forward, she whispered in Mini's ear. 'Heard the latest? Mumbai office has a new production head!'

Mini was all ears. Gossip! She loooved it! 'What's her name? Where is she from?'

Deepa winked. 'It's a *he*! And he's a bawa!'

'Parsi dheekra? Su chheh!'

Deepa leaned even closer. 'He has been hired by Mahatta because Soul Mates has landed a big one! A Rajput prince is getting married to a Bollywood starlet in Mumbai. No budget, that's what the groom's father told Mahatta. He wants to host the grandest show on Earth – something exceptional, something his guests would have never seen before. It's going to be the talk of the town. I wish I was going, but Mahatta will only want you to go. You better send me a running commentary,' said Deepa, stars in her eyes.

Mini waved her hand in front of Deepa's face, trying to shake her out of her trance. 'I'm not going! I hate travelling, you know that. And more than that, I hate aeroplanes. And then, fending for myself in Mumbai! Sorry, I can't do this, I'm too old.'

'Old? You are the craziest, wackiest person in the company!' Deepa replied.

Mini gave her a disbelieving look and opened her lunch box, revealing the wilted salad she had made in the morning. Deepa opened her box, taking out still-warm aloo paranthas with oily mango pickle. Mini's mouth watered. Deepa looked at Mini's lunch. 'Dieting again?' she asked. Putting a parantha dripping with mango-flavored oil in a plate, she turned to Mini. 'Eat na, one parantha won't make any difference. Besides, thin won't suit you. You look so cuddly and mommy-like, the way you are. Come on, eat up!'

'No way,' Mini protested. 'I'm not touching that stuff.' But her hand moved on its own volition. Mini had no say in the matter. Disgusted with herself, Mini ate the parantha, followed it up with cake and then drowned her sorrows in a cola. Cute, plump, motherly ... that's what she would always be, she mused glumly. Why even try to be someone else?

Deepa cut into her thoughts. 'Have you been to the doctor yet? Sometimes, weight gain can be hormonal; you better get a check-up.'

Mini nodded. She had an appointment in a few days. Her periods had been erratic for the past few months. Hopefully, it was nothing serious, like the dreaded C word. Cervical cancer! God, no! She sent up a silent prayer. Please don't make me have cervical cancer. I will be really good from now on – no cigarettes, no beer and no paranthas. No erotic thoughts about Mills & Boon heroes.

\* \* \*

It was a slow week, work-wise. With plenty of free time on their hands, Mini and Deepa gossiped to their hearts' content. The new manager in Mumbai was the hot topic of discussion. They wondered if he was married. Deepa tried to check him out on Facebook but drew a blank; privacy settings took all the fun out of stalking. Deepa was convinced the man was gay as only gay men joined the wedding business. Mini wondered what he was being paid and decided to throttle Mahatta if he was paying the gay Parsi more than she was.

The socialite dropped by, wanting to see possible designs for her wedding dress. Mini showed her sketches of the magenta-and-yellow balloon pants with the gold brocade coat, done by the in-house designer. They discussed details like décor, music and choreography. The socialite got so carried away by the idea of hot-air balloons, she wanted them for the entire baraat. Mini could see the prospective wedding procession in her mind's eye. It would be a spectacular sight. A hundred hot-air balloons, decorated to kill, floating above the city's skyline. It would be a dream exercise for the creative team and a nightmare for the production guys. Which made it perfect, Mini thought, anticipating the war ahead.

In the evening, Deepa and Mini were on site-supervision duty in West Delhi. It was a conventional wedding, for the scion of a nouveau riche family. Mini had arranged so many, she could conjure one up with her eyes closed. A huge marquee had been set up. Men in Soul Mates uniforms were busy stuffing flowers into huge metal tubs. A mechanism with hosepipes would be attached to the tubs and petals would be pumped up. As the bride and groom took their pheras, roses would shower on their heads like blessings.

Workers atop high ladders were fixing strings of orchids to the marquee roof and entrance. Large red and gold bows were being tied to the backs of chairs. In another area, two massive thrones were being offloaded from a van while vases with red roses were being placed on tables covered with muted gold tablecloths.

Mini and Deepa stood on one side, indifferent to the chaos, absorbed in conversation. Deepa was venting against her husband of seven years. 'So I've told him, it's either her or me. He has to choose. But if he chooses to divorce me, I'll take him to the cleaners,' she said.

'Oh no, I left the dry cleaner's bill at home! Shyam is going to grouch like crazy,' Mini remembered.

Deepa ignored the irrelevant remark. 'I don't know why I put up with him. I should never have married him,' she lamented.

Mini nodded wisely. 'Experience has taught me that marriage is a huge con, an illusion, my dear. And yet, we all get into it. Give me romance any day and once the romance wears off, give me ... another romance!' she declared. Deepa laughed, and then frowned as her mobile phone rang and her husband's name blinked on the screen. She moved away to talk in privacy.

An old lady was walking in their direction. 'You are the wedding planners?' she wanted to know.

'Yes, Ma'am,' Mini replied. 'You must be the bride's grandmother?' she queried.

'Yes, but next month I'm going to be the bride!' the old lady said as she smiled, revealing flawless false teeth.

'You! I mean ... congratulations, Ma'am!' Mini piped up, trying hard to hide her skepticism. Deepa had finished her phone call and was standing behind the lady, listening incredulously.

'Third-time-lucky, I'm hoping! So ... I wanted to ask, will you plan the wedding?' the old lady asked, coyly.

'Certainly, Ma'am. Once you've decided on the date, I'll check our calendar and let you know. Just call me tomorrow and we'll make an appointment?' Mini said, politely, handing a Soul Mates visiting card to the lady.

'Thank you dear. See you later, I have to go get my hair done now. *He* will be coming!' the lady said coquettishly, as she hurried off.

'What hair?' Deepa demanded to know. 'She's got all of three strands. I counted!' She shook her head. 'Third time! Some women are suckers for punishment.'

'Oh no, women are suckers only for romance!' Mini retorted.

They could have carried on the discussion forever, but the brass band started to rehearse, declaring the topic closed.

\* \* \*

Mini was briefing the art department on designs for hot-air balloons when Mahatta summoned her to his cabin. He was on the phone when she entered. Mini sat down, idly thinking that Mahatta would make a great Bollywood villain. He looked like the poor man's Mogambo, complete with oily, hennaed hair, arranged in careful locks on the forehead. The golden buttons on his safari suit completed the look, she mused.

Mini gathered from the conversation that Mahatta was talking to the gay Parsi. He put the phone down and turned to Mini. 'Our Mumbai branch needs a creative person Mrinaliniji. I told them I'd send my best. So how would you like to relocate temporarily to Mumbai, Mrinaliniji? Just for a few months? It is for a great, royal wedding, and there are no limits on the budget! Can you imagine Mrinaliniji? *No budget*! What an opportunity, Mrinaliniji!' He looked at her owlishly through his glasses. 'Aapka ticket kab kay liye book karoon?'

Mini was thrown into confusion. It would be a challenging assignment. But accepting it was out of the question. She was not going to give up her diet, her plans to work out and the makeover appointment she had decided to fix for next week. She had a strategy and going to Mumbai would be most inopportune.

'Sir, I would love to go but … Polka – our dog – is unwell and I just cannot leave. I'm sorry, Sir.'

Mahatta did not look too happy about Mini's response. 'Think about it Mrinaliniji. I forgot to mention that this will mean a direct raise in salary, by 30 per cent … er … 40 per cent. So let me know tomorrow. Talk to Shyam. He will want you to go, I'm sure. He can also join you in Mumbai for some time. Soul Mates will take care of the expenses...'

Mini was shocked at this never-seen-before streak of generosity. They must need her really bad in Mumbai!

It was turning out to be a happy day after all. Aditi, Mini's childhood boarding-school buddy, was in town from Mumbai. They had agreed to meet up for a beer in the evening at a restaurant near the office. Hugging and squealing loudly, they met like two schoolgirls, much to the amusement of the young couple at the next table. Aditi was glowing with a healthy tan; she had just come back from a holiday in Bali. Mini marveled at her. She was one gutsy girl. Imagine going for a holiday all by yourself. Mini could never think of doing that.

'Didn't you get frightened, all alone?' she asked.

'Mini, you should try it. It's fantastic! Nobody knows you, no one bothers you, and you can be whoever you want to be. It is so liberating! I flirted with a different guy every day!'

Mini was intrigued. Maybe this was what she needed, some 'me-time', away from husband and home. She could pretend to be single and who knows, meet Dream Lover! She made a mental note to look up likely destinations on Google. Bali was out because Mini hated flying. It would have to be some place within driving distance.

Aditi asked her about work and Mini told her about the Great Royal Wedding and Mahatta's offer. Aditi urged her to take it. 'You can stay with me. Surekha, Kirti, Dhira, Bhavna, Indranie, Shradha, Nandita ... they are all in Mumbai, it will be like old times!'

Mini promised to think about it, but in her heart, she knew she didn't have the courage. Aditi could do it; she had lived alone for years. Mini herself was a real scaredy-cat. For one, she couldn't sleep alone; the merest sound spooked her. Once when Shyam had to go out of town for his uncle's funeral, she had spent the entire night sitting up, imagining that the uncle's ghost was lurking behind the curtain. That's when Shyam had brought Polka home and appointed her as Mini's personal bodyguard and companion. No, she would never be comfortable or happy alone. DL would have to be a Delhi Lad after all.

All through the next day at work, Mahatta kept asking her to change her mind. His open praise for her talent made Mini feel wonderful inside. It was great to feel wanted and appreciated. She was the best and there was no better wedding planner in the world than her; she rejoiced silently. Lulled into a good mood, she decided that she would be extra nice to Shyam and then maybe he too would learn to appreciate her.

Mini stopped on the way back from work, to buy ingredients for gajar ka halwa. It was Shyam's favourite dessert. At home, she changed the tablecloth and laid the table with her best cutlery. Washing and polishing a crystal vase, she cut pink, fragrant roses from the garden and arranged them. And when the clock chimed eight, she lit a scented candle and placed it at the centre of the table.

She was in the kitchen, garnishing the gajar ka halwa with pistachios, when he came home, looking like a dark omen. He stormed upstairs, glaring at her as he muttered darkly to himself. Mini wondered what could be bothering him. Could it be something she had done? A business snafu, she conjectured, hoping that whatever it was would be taken care of by dum aloo. The way to this man's heart was through his stomach, she knew. One look at the buffet she had laid out and he would start purring.

Half an hour later, he came to the dinner table, still glowering.

'Hi. Something the matter? Business trouble?' Mini asked, trying to inject wifely concern into her voice. He didn't reply. Looking pointedly at the roses in the vase, Mini waited for him to appreciate her efforts. 'We can talk about it later, Honey. Come, let's enjoy our dinner,' Mini murmured softly, picking up the dum aloo dish and spooning some into his plate.

Shyam sat there like a statue, staring at the steaming gravy. Mini got up, went to his side of the table and lovingly lifted a spoonful to his mouth.

He came down on her like a ton of bricks. Fishing out some papers from his pocket, he thrust them under her nose. Mini's heart sank. Were those challans? So many? She was D.E.A.D. Glaring at her like her childhood Math tutor, Shyam started his tirade. 'Business troubles? Ha! Those are nothing compared to the havoc you can cause, Mini! Jumping three red lights on the same day? Congratulations, very few people manage that. Quite a feat! Even for you!'

Mini decided that offence was the best defense. 'In fifteen years, have you learnt to pick up the toilet seat? Or to stop snoring?' she retorted.

Shyam turned red, anger oozing from every pore. 'So? I admit I'm not perfect, but at least I don't come running to you for every small thing. "Shyam, I have a puncture, please get it fixed." "Please Shyam, get the flush in the loo repaired, please na!" You can't even take a crap without me! But this time you go and pay your own damn challans! I'm not going to do this for you! Got it?'

That stung. Mini lashed out. 'But that's what husbands are for! To carry suitcases, hammer nails, fix the cable TV ... if you can't even do these chores, what's the point of having a husband?

As it is, you've become Shyam Bhaiyya lately. I might as well look for someone else!'

Things were getting out of hand. Shyam was in a fine fettle by now. 'Who can make love to a bag of cellulite?' he shouted.

'Who wants a jiggly paunch and man-boobs?' Mini shot back.

The fight would have become uglier, but Shyam's phone rang. Saved by the bell, Mini thought, watching his expression change as tenderness swept his features.

'Are you sure? When is the delivery going to happen? How many babies, can you tell? And is my Polka in good health? Thank you, thank you! Congratulations to you too!' Shyam's anger evaporated. The call was from their friendly neighbourhood vet. Shyam and Mini were going to be grandparents. Their golden retriever's litter was on the way!

Shyam totally forgot about the quarrel, so happy was he about Polka's good news. But Mini was rather upset. How could Shyam be so cruel? Mini could take many things in her stride but she drew the line at references to her weight. Calling her a bag of cellulite was hitting below the belt. Wasn't she dieting? Hadn't she decided to join the gym, for heaven's sake? As if Shyam himself looked like George Clooney. More like Danny DeVito, she thought, watching him wolf down gajar ka halwa like it was going out of style.

Why did she even bother, Mini berated herself. Every time she went out of her way to rekindle the romance with Shyam, she fell flat on her face. And god knows, she tried. Okay, so Shyam was not the roses-and-sonnets type, but how difficult could it be to part with a word of appreciation now and then? A compliment, once in a while? He barely looked at her any more and the only dialogue they had was over the phone, in monosyllables. What kind of meaningless farce had their relationship become, where they could no longer have an intimate conversation, leave alone intimacy in bed? Naturally she had begun to feel incomplete, starved as she was of attention, love and understanding. Even her self-image had taken a major hit, she realized. What was the point of looking good if the man in your life didn't care two hoots? Might as well eat and grow fatter, Mini thought, a tear rolling down her cheek. She was never going to try again, Mini promised herself. Shyam was history. She was going to replace him with someone who cared.

Too distraught to read, Mini switched on the television. A Michael Douglas film, *The War of the Roses*, was being aired on Star Movies. It seemed to match Mini's current frame of mind. She got so absorbed in the film, she barely looked up when Shyam came into the room and got into bed. It was bizarre. Kathleen Turner and Michael Douglas were going at each other, hammer and tongs. They were pretty violent too. Mini got a little carried away. When Shyam let out a loud snore, she grabbed a cushion and pressed it down hard on his face. Shyam gasped for breath.

'You snore once more and I swear, I'll kill you,' Mini said, and meant it.

Shyam didn't even open his eyes. He shoved the cushion aside and went back to sleep, leaving Mini utterly defeated as the anger drained out of her. Did life never imitate the movies? Why was Shyam so passive? On its own volition, her hand searched for the diet chocolate under the mattress. Shakespeare had got it wrong. Mini knew from years of experience, it wasn't sleep that was the balm for hurt minds; it was chocolate.

★ ★ ★

The gynaecologist's clinic was in Connaught Place and parking was going to be a nightmare. But Mini was lucky for once. She found a slot right outside the clinic gate. It was a marvel how the place wasn't taken. She picked up the envelope containing her test results and sailed in.

A young man with oily hair was sitting in the doctor's cabin. He introduced himself as Dr Ganapathy's new assistant. Mini was taken aback. She wasn't sure she could handle being examined by a male doctor ... not until she had lost some weight.

Dr Ganapathy walked in five minutes later, resplendent in a gorgeous Kanjeevaram. She glanced at the tests and looked thoughtfully at Mini. 'How old are you now, Mini?'

'Er ... forty-ish,' Mini replied.

'There is nothing I can see that is wrong with you. Erratic periods have several causes, and the tests have ruled out all, except one. You are heading for menopause.'

*Menopause*? Mini froze.

'But that's something that happens to women in their mid-fifties! I am too young! There must be some mistake!' Mini exclaimed.

Dr Ganapathy shook her head. 'These days menopause is happening earlier. It's because of all the lifestyle changes, you see. Smoking, drinking, no exercise, obesity ... it's happening to a lot of women your age, even younger.'

Mini was in a state of shock. 'What's going to happen to me, Doctor?'

Dr Ganapathy reeled out the list of symptoms and effects. 'Hot flushes, irregular periods, dry skin, hair fall, loss of libido...' She stopped when she saw the stricken expression on Mini's face. 'Come on Mrinalini! Don't get so frightened. Basically, menopause signals the end of your child-bearing years. It's like a coming of age, a signal.'

A signal of what, of the end coming nigh, Mini wondered, in despair. 'It tells you that you are ready to move away from the carnal to the spiritual. You are finally free of romance and infatuations and can turn your mind to divine love!'

Mini almost fainted. Dr Ganapathy carried on regardless. 'It can be wonderful, I can tell you. It's just another phase of life. A lot of women welcome it! This is simply nature's way of preparing you for grandchildren. And imagine never having to worry about staining your Kanjeevaram silks! I've been through it and I vouch for it. Nothing like the freedom menopause gives you!'

Mini couldn't take it any more. She excused herself, got up in a daze, paid at the reception and went towards the car park. Where was it? Her car had vanished into thin air! Should she ring up the police?

Frantically, she pulled out her phone and called Shyam. He sounded irritated. 'Go to the nearest police station, it must have been towed away.'

She begged him to come and rescue her but he flatly refused. India and Pakistan were playing a match and he was not going to budge, even if his wife was traumatized. Why was she the last in Shyam's list of priorities? First, he cared about himself; second, the dog; third, the TV; fourth, the Internet; fifth, his buddies. She was lucky if she got into the first hundred, Mini thought bitterly.

She looked around helplessly, trying to spot an auto-rickshaw. Instead, she saw her car, barely visible, behind an oversized SUV. It had been parked in such a tight spot. She didn't remember manoeuvring it, though. Loss of memory was one of the signs of menopause, the doctor had said. Or was it loss of libido? Most likely it was both, Mini thought gloomily.

Mini somehow reversed the car on to the road, still in a daze over her impending menopause. Her mind raced as she pressed the accelerator. How could it arrive so early? It was so unfair. She had so many unfulfilled fantasies, and now she was going to end up a married old maid. That Shyam was not going to fulfill them for her, was a foregone conclusion. Shyam was a habit. And romance was by nature, exotic and anticipative. She was fat but she too had romantic feelings. She could feel them in her bones. It was a different matter that she couldn't feel her bones. Life had never looked so bleak.

She drove slowly, lost in thought, but she had to stop a few metres ahead. The car was making a strange, knocking noise. Mini was alarmed. She knew next to nothing about cars. Shyam had once told the mechanic that his car's engine was knocking. She ought to check, Mini knew, but she didn't have a clue how to open the bonnet.

It wasn't the engine. A strange man was knocking at her window. Mini accelerated as though the demons were after her. Delhi was the rape capital of the country, everyone said. She raced. A quick glance at the rear-view mirror had her shuddering over a speed breaker, almost breaking the car into two. The man was chasing her, running wildly, waving his arms in a demented way. Mini swerved into a lane, demolished a hedge, broke through a dhobi's clothesline and finally slammed home.

There were two other cars parked outside the house when she reached home. That meant Shyam's friends were over as usual. Mini wanted to tell Shyam about her narrow escape from the rapist but with his cricket-crazy friends around, she wasn't going to get his attention. Here she was, on the verge of menopause, and all that these men could do was watch cricket. They must be glued to something meaningless, like those IPL thingies. Why were men so fixated on cricket, she wondered. As if any of those hunky players cared for Mr Sicko Shyam's opinions. They didn't even know he existed. A one-sided affair, if there ever was one.

Mini was about to tiptoe to her room, intending to research menopause when she heard a blood-curdling yell from the TV room. She ran, imagining Shyam being murdered by his cronies. She had heard some ominous stuff about cricket betting lately. Inside, she was greeted by the sight of three grown men staring at the television as though about to burst into tears. They scarcely looked up when she entered. 'Er … what's the score?' she asked, tentatively.

'India needs twenty runs to win. Four balls to go,' Shyam replied, without taking his eyes off the screen.

'And who's batting?' she asked, trying hard to look interested.

Three pairs of male eyes turned to her in unison, their expressions a mix of incredulity and rage. Mini beat a hasty retreat.

Should she tell Shyam about the street Romeo? More importantly, should she tell him about menopause, Mini wondered as she changed into her nightclothes. In all probability, he would just make fun of her; sensitivity was not his strong point. Plus, it was not as if she had reached menopause already. There were things to be accomplished. Mini dug out the facial cream that had been lying in the bathroom cabinet for over a year, and smeared it on. 'Everyoung.. Great name, hope it lives up to it, Mini thought. Climbing into bed with a stack of magazines, she proceeded to cut out every write-up she could find for younger skin, makeovers, Botox clinics and instant slimming cures. As the mask hardened and caked on her face, she noted phone numbers, stuffed some cuttings into her bag and finally, turned to the bookmarked page on her paperback romance.

She was just getting cozy when the doorbell rang. Mini cursed cricket. No way was Shyam going to answer the bell. She would have to get up. It was probably the chowkidar wanting to know the score.

Mini couldn't believe her eyes. Standing outside, was the roadside Romeo. He was staring at her as if he was looking at a ghost. She was about to deliver all the Punjabi abuses she knew when he spoke. 'Ma'am, you drove away with my car.'

The man didn't speak like roadside Romeo. Mini stared. Suddenly she remembered where she had seen him. It was the junior doctor from Dr Ganapathy's clinic. Had she driven away in his car? An irreverent giggle rose up in Mini's stomach, but it morphed into alarm. 'Where is *my* car then?' she asked.

'At the clinic, Ma'am. If you give me my car keys, I will drive you back to yours.'

Her car was there, right next to the gate, standing alone and forlorn, in the dark. Everyone else had gone home. The lone guard gave her strange looks and a wide berth. Well, she deserved that, Mini thought. Who in their right minds drove off in someone else's car? Maybe her subconscious mind had reacted to menopause by mixing up cars. Mini thought hard as she drove home. She needed to get away, before she completely lost it. But where could she go?

Had she been brave, she could have gone to Bali alone, like Aditi.

Wait a minute, this was it! She could take up Mahatta's offer! In a flash, Mini's mood shifted gear, from melancholy to euphoria. She began to quickly plan ahead. In Mumbai, she could stay with Aditi, so no question of being alone. She could do this! Mini straightened her spine. She was not giving in. She was going to get her share of romance, and get it before menopause set in. She was going to fulfill her wildest fantasies, in seventy-millimetre, grand, Hollywood style. First, she was going to lose weight. Next, she was going to get a new wardrobe and a complete makeover. Then she was going to give Shyam the slip and go to Mumbai and wait for DL to appear. And he would. She was not going to concede to menopause.

Screw menopause, she screamed out loud, making heads turn in the rush-hour traffic. She laughed in defiance and raced home, jumping another red light.

She didn't know when she fell asleep but she was woken up by a shriek. It was Shyam, pretending to be spooked by her face mask. The mask! She had forgotten all about it. Mini leapt to the bathroom. And shrieked. A half made-up geisha stared back at her. She had driven to the clinic and back, looking like a demented harridan.

If Shyam had bothered to talk to her or at least look at her instead of being glued to the TV, he could have warned her not to go out of the house without washing the mask off. Now she would be the laughing stock of the entire neighbourhood. Shyam was still guffawing … she could hear him through the bathroom door. Sicko Shyam. Always ready to make her feel worse when she was low. She brushed her teeth, sat down on the WC and took out a chocolate from its hiding place in the towel shelf. She was not going to let Sicko Shyam stop her. She was going to be slim and beautiful and he was going to come panting after her. And then, she was going to laugh as she roared away into the Magical Mumbai sunset on DL's arm.

Ha ha ha! Mini got into bed with her romance novel and was soon lost between its torrid sheets.

\* \* \*

Deepa accosted Mini the minute she entered the office. She was bursting with breaking news.

Mahatta had given the Mumbai assignment to their arch-enemy, Sonal, who came across to Mini's table, looking like the proverbial cat that had licked all the cream.

'I knew you wouldn't want to go, so I thought – let me do this one! Mumbai is a young peoples' city, you know. I just love it! You would probably feel like a fish out of water there ... and Rustom ... you know, the Mumbai manager? He has specifically asked for someone youthful and energetic...' she trailed off meaningfully.

Mini saw red. Before she knew what she was doing, she was in Mahatta's office. Without waiting for him to speak, she blurted out. 'Sir, I am ready to go to Mumbai. You can book my ticket.'

Mahatta looked nonplussed. 'But I booked Sonal's. She will be very disappointed.'

Mini squared her shoulders. 'So cancel Sonal's ticket. I am the only one who can pull off a project as big as this one, you know that.' Mahatta looked at her like a trapped animal. Mini was past caring by now. This was the perfect opportunity to teach Sicko Shyam a lesson; she wasn't going to pass it on, that too, to Sonal.

A shaken Mahatta picked up the phone and spoke to the travel agent. Mini looked at him and grinned inwardly. Poor Mahatta, she thought. He looked traumatized, caught as he was between Smouldering Sonal and Mad Mini. Well, he would have to find a way to appease Sonal.

'Sir, maybe Sonal could go to the Jat wedding coming up in Bhatinda?' she asked him, tongue firmly in cheek. Mahatta sighed as he called Mumbai to tell the office about Mini's arrival.

Mini walked out, head held high in triumph. Sonal took one look at her and ran to Mahatta's cabin. Mini made a victory sign at Deepa who answered with a gleeful thumbs-up. Nobody liked Sonal. Mini felt less guilty about ruining Sonal's plans. Everything was fair in menopause and war, she thought, steeling her resolve.

It was done. She would go to Mumbai. That night, Mini found herself daydreaming. Maybe Mumbai would prove to be the Promised Land? She could cultivate a new self, project a new image, even have an affair? That would serve Sicko Shyam right. And who knew, may be the Parsi wasn't gay after all? She could ask Mahatta but he would probably say something like 'Mrinaliniji, aap kya poochch raheen hain? Gay toh hai woh, bada khush rehta hai, jaisey main hoon, happy and gay!' Yes, this was her chance – the last dash of romance before menopause came knocking, Mini thought. Tomorrow she would shop for her new look, she determined as she fell asleep.

Shyam came in after the 10.00 p.m. news and found her asleep with glasses on, book on her chest, mouth open. He placed the book and glasses on the side table, patted her cheek tenderly and went to bed.

\* \* \*

Mini had taken the day off, telling Mahatta that she had to cook and freeze Shyam's meals before she could take off to Mumbai. Mahatta looked at her as if she was a goddess. 'A career woman who can cook and freeze! Mrinaliniji, you are great!' She could read his mind as he readily obliged.

Her first step was the store for designer dresses where Sonal shopped. She asked for short dresses in her size. The sales woman handed her an extra-large size. Mini requested for a medium size; she was going on a diet so she had to invest in her future size. She picked up skirts in several colours, matching blouses and a long dress in bold purple. The long dress was a large size, to wear while she was still losing weight.

The next stop was the lingerie store. Here she went a little berserk, shunning the plain, practical whites she normally bought and going in for lacy wisps of nothing. And then, as if to tempt fate, she added a naughty red negligeé, guaranteed to make a humdrum homemaker look like somebody's mistress. She was satisfied for the time being, the rest she could buy in Mumbai.

There was something else that Mini was looking forward to, on reaching Mumbai. Her old boarding-school friends were there – five of them. She could meet them after years and yet, when she did, it always felt like no time had passed. They had known each other since they were in Nursery. All of them were the same age, had started their period at the same time, got married roughly in the same year, and now even their children were around the same age. Except, of course, Aditi, who had chosen to not marry. It would be great to catch up with the gang, Mini thought. They were the only people on Earth with whom she could share her true feelings. Agree or disagree, they would be with her in whatever decision she took. Nothing like school friends, Mini thought, as she drove home, waving out cheekily at the traffic policeman as she raced through the red light. Let him challan me, Mini thought. Sicko Shyam will have to deal with it, because she was leaving on a jet plane! The revenge was already happening. And soon, Sicko Shyam would have to cope with shopping, buying groceries, dealing with the dhobi, the maali and a pregnant dog … all on his own!

But just when she thought she had Shyam all figured out, he came up with a surprise. She had assumed he would be happy to have her out of his hair for some months. But here he was, refusing to let her go! They were having a leisurely Sunday breakfast when she broke the news to him.

'How can you just leave me and go?' he whined, full of reproach.

Mini was at a loss. This was the last thing she had expected. 'Why can't you manage without me? There is a full-time maid; she'll cook whatever you order. The dhobi will do the laundry. And, if you get lonely, you can visit your parents,' she said.

But Shyam was adamant. 'You are *not* going, and that's that. Alone in Mumbai for so long? You must be mad! You want the marriage to break up or what?' he thundered.

Mini was piqued. 'What marriage? You call this a marriage? When was the last time you looked at me properly? Or paid me a compliment? Or brought me flowers on our anniversary?'

Shyam looked guiltily at his egg, sunny-side down. 'It was yesterday, in case you were wondering.' Mini walked away in a huff, leaving Shyam staring after her helplessly.

Mini relished her little victory but she hadn't won the war yet. How was she going to get Shyam to let her go to Mumbai? She decided to try a softer, more devious approach. Slipping into a fresh salwar-kameez, she doused perfume and put on some war paint – lipstick, kajal, a little rouge, nothing too obvious. Downstairs, Shyam was still staring morosely at his egg.

Standing behind his chair, Mini put her arms around him and muttered into his ear. 'Okay, sorry. I hate fighting with you.'

Shyam looked up hopefully. 'Me too,' he murmured into his beard.

'It's okay, I won't go to Mumbai. Not when it's upsetting you so much,' Mini crooned.

Shyam puffed up. He pulled her around, on to his large lap. They sat in companionable silence for a while as Mini bided her time. 'You know, Mahatta is offering a 40 per cent raise with this move. But what do I care about money? You're more important than a few lakh rupees, right?'

Shyam squirmed uncomfortably. '40 per cent raise? Maybe we should think about it.'

Mini smirked inwardly. 'No no, Sonal will go.'

'Yeah, let her,' Shyam replied, sounding a little unsure, rocking her slowly on his lap.

'I'll get passed up for a promotion. But that's the least I can do for you,' Mini continued silkily. Shyam's ears stood up. 'After completing this assignment, Sonal will become my boss. But who cares?' Mini purred. 'I'll have to quit my job. But we will live on one salary, along with love and fresh air,' Mini finished.

Shyam bristled. 'What? That Mahatta! I'll see how that Sonal gets your promotion! You are going to Mumbai, and *that* is final!'

Mini bit her cheek to hide her exultant smile. Husbands! They were so predictable! Giving Shyam a peck on his chin, Mini raced upstairs to pack, Shyam following slowly. She was putting her clothes in the suitcase when Shyam peeped in, a hangdog expression on his face.

'When do you have to leave?' he asked.

'Tomorrow evening,' she replied, trying hard to keep the excitement out of her voice.

'Where will you stay in Mumbai?' Shyam wanted to know.

'Mahatta is paying for hotel accommodation but I'll probably move into Aditi's.'

'Which hotel? Is it near the Soul Mates office?' Shyam asked.

'I haven't had time to check.' Mini replied, absently.

'Our neighbours have a hotel in Andheri. If you don't like your hotel, you call Pritam Pal, okay?' Shyam said.

'Sure, remind me to take the phone number before I go,' Mini replied, as she continued to pack, not at all interested in contacting anyone. Quickly, she put all her new dresses in the suitcase, leaving the red negligeé to the last. Shyam picked it up.

'What's this for?' he asked suspiciously.

'Oh, that? That's a gift for Aditi,' Mini lied.

'For Aditi? When did she get a man in her life?' Shyam asked.

'She doesn't have a man in her life. That is precisely why I'm giving it to her,' Mini fibbed.

Shyam looked baffled but seemed to swallow the lie. He shuffled out of the room. Mini continued packing, picking up a dozen or more of her favourite romances and packing them next to her CDs. Her choice in music was thumris, sung in shringaar ras. She adored them, even though they filled her with disquiet and longing. Next came her high-heeled shoes and sandals. She wore them only on occasions, but in Mumbai, she planned to make every moment a celebration.

'Two days more, where will I be, out of gates of matrimony!' Mini hummed the line tunelessly as she packed.

Shyam emerged from the dressing room just as she was about to shut the suitcase. He had a framed picture in his hand. Mini and Shyam together, his arm around her, both looking happy. It was an old photograph, taken on Shyam's birthday a few years ago. Shyam carefully packed the frame in bubble wrap and placed it in the suitcase. It sat there on top of the naughty negligeé, waiting to play witness to the guilty adventures that lay in store for her.

# 2

―――

Mumbai's newly renovated airport gave Mini the heebie-jeebies. She felt lost and apprehensive. What if the Mumbai office hadn't sent anyone to pick her up? How would she find her way to the hotel? If only Shyam was with her. He always took care of cabs, luggage and stuff like that. Mini caught herself just in time. How could she want Shyam here, when she was looking for her last tango in Mumbai? This was *her* time; she wasn't going to have Shyam spoil it. She squared her shoulders and tried to look confident.

An effeminate man in floral trousers and dramatic make-up was looking in her direction. Finally, Mini thought, the gay Parsi! She walked up to him and enquired, 'Soul Mates?'

'Darling, no offence, but you're not my type!' he tittered. Mini was about to give him a piece of her mind when she felt a tap on her shoulder.

Turning around, she saw a Greek god. He looked like he had just walked out of one of her romantic novels. Surely he wasn't looking for her?

'Mrs Mehta? I am Rustom from Soul Mates. May I take your bags?'

Mini stared. And kept on staring. Ohmygosh, he was carrying

a bouquet of roses! Were they for her? They were! Unbelievable! Wordlessly, Mini handed her laptop and suitcase to the god and followed him to his car, clutching the bouquet. Wonder of wonders, the god opened the door for her and held it while she slipped in! Mini was stupefied. This hadn't happened to her since the days Shyam had courted her.

The god started the car and they moved into the sultry Mumbai evening. 'I trust the flight was comfortable, Mrs Mehta?' the god enquired, head bent deferentially to one side.

'It's Mini to my friends,' Mini spoke, as she finally found her voice.

'Is the air conditioning too much? I can turn it down if you're cold,' the god said, fussing over her, making her feel like a queen.

'Just a little, maybe,' Mini said, in a husky, Marilyn-Monroe drawl. Rustom turned down the AC and flipped on the CD player. Soft, romantic violin strains filled the car. Mini was encouraged but cautious. Could it be that he found her attractive or was he this solicitous with every woman he met?

'I am so glad you were able to come and help out on the royal wedding. You and I will make a great team, I'm sure,' Rustom said.

'You and I? Certainly, we could make a really hot team,' Mini said, fluttering her eyelashes. The god didn't bat an eyelid.

'So, what does a single girl do in your town in the evenings?' Mini asked.

Rustom turned into a quiet lane. 'Whatever she likes. There are plenty of eating places, pubs, lounges, bars...'

'Are you inviting me to dinner?' Mini asked, giving him a coy look.

'I would have loved to, Mrs Mehta ... sorry ... Mini, but I can't, not tonight.'

'Got a heavy date lined up?' said Mini, trying hard not to look put out.

'No, it's just that my wife is waiting for me at home.'

'A married man? Interesting!' Mini replied, trying to keep the disappointment out of her tone.

Rustom stopped at a suburban hotel and called the gateman to take Mini's bags. He opened the door for her once again, waiting politely till she had safely disembarked. 'Welcome to Mumbai! I will see you at the office tomorrow!'

The old Mini resurfaced in a panic. 'Office? I don't where it is! How does one get there?'

'I'll pick you up, you're on my way. Not a problem. Be ready, I'll be here at 9.00 a.m. sharp. Good night!' Rustom drove away, leaving Mini in a swirl of after-shave.

He's dishy. Let's just hope he isn't served gay, Mini thought. He was also married. He could be a gay husband or a straight philanderer. Could he possibly be DL?

Well done Mini, she congratulated herself. You've met a Greek god on your first day in Mumbai! Anything could happen in a few months ... and she was more than game.

* * *

Mini was in fine form. She imagined herself to be a heroine from one of her bolder romances. Ensconced in her room, she had a long, languorous soak, emptying an entire bottle of bubble-bath foam into the tub. Then she squeezed into her new dress, sprayed perfume, ditched her glasses, double mascaraed her eyes and slipped on slinky, high-heeled sandals. Not bad, she thought, as she squinted, short-sightedly, at herself in the mirror. She looked well endowed, but sexy. Heads would turn tonight, she was certain.

Tottering to the hotel's garden bar, she perched herself on a high bar stool. From her bag, she pulled out an ultra-slim cigarette, bought at the Delhi airport. The bartender politely held a lit match. She cupped her hand around his, inhaled and blew smoke into his face. Somehow, it ended up going into her eyes, reducing her sight to zero visibility. Unfazed, she leaned forward and ordered a drink. 'A single malt, large.'

Waiting for her drink, Mini surveyed the room through her mascaraed, smoke-filled gaze, every inch the femme fatale, in predatory mode. The drink appeared; Mini tossed it back with a flourish. The world grew hazier. She could just about make out a tall man in a hat, sitting a few tables away, staring at her. Mini was thrilled. The bold new Mini was a hit! She asked for a refill. When she peeked discreetly again, the man was still staring at her. She grew more daring. Asking the waiter for a slip of paper, she scrawled, 'Would you like to join me for a drink?' on it and told him to hand it to the gentleman. She saw the man receiving the note and yes! He was walking towards her! Mini quickly flicked a lock of hair in front of her eyes and twisted her lips into a sexy pout. The man was almost behind her now.

'Bhabhiji! Aap hi hain? Yahaan? Where is Shyam?'

Mini cringed. It couldn't be. But it was. Their neighbour, the crass Punjabi, Pritam Pal Singh. She flung the cigarette away and desperately swallowed the smoke. The cigarette landed on a pile of napkins at the bar which started to burn. The conflagration grew alarmingly. A smoke alarm started to beep. Someone emptied an ice bucket on the fire, drenching the counter and Mini's front. She leapt off the bar stool, tripping over her dress. Staff came running from all directions. Pritam hurriedly whisked Mini away to the lobby.

Mini was on the verge of asking Pritam what he was doing in Mumbai when she remembered. Pritam was a hotelier. Shyam had mentioned that he had bought a hotel in Mumbai lately. Rotten luck, Mini thought despondently. Out of all the hotels she could have stayed in, Soul Mates had to put her up in the one owned by Sardar Pritam Pal.

'Sweetie is also here, and both the children. I own the hotel, you know, na? Sweetie wanted to do some shopping-vopping and the bachchaas wanted to go to the beach-sheech, so I thought, why not? Ab toh stay is free in Mumbai! Te Shyam kiththey hai?' he rambled, without pause.

'Shyam is in Delhi. I am here on work,' Mini said, her eyes trying to focus through running mascara.

'So you are alone? Worry not, we are here! I'll tell Shyam, yeh koi baat hui, bhabhi ko akeley bhej diya? Aur aap kaisey aa gaye ussey chhod kay? You can't be too careful, Bhabhiji. Never leave your spouse alone like this. Kissi aur pay dil aa gaya, toh?' Pritam sniggered at his own joke. 'Chalo, you are having dinner with us. In the rooftop restaurant. It's called "The Great Indian Family". My Pinkoo named it ... you like?'

Mini desperately tried to get out of the dinner plan. 'Dinner? But I'm not dressed for a family-type place,' she protested.

Pritam nodded. 'Yes, they don't allow nighties. You go and change and we will meet in fifteen minutes in the restaurant. Okay, Bhabhiji?'

Mini nodded miserably and crept away towards the lift. This is perfect, she thought. Her seduction plan involved Sardar Pritam Pal. Her slinky, new dress was a nightie. The sultry-siren act was a damp squib. And her hot dinner date was in a restaurant called 'The Great Indian Family'. Mini resigned herself to her fate as she washed her face, wriggled into a demure salwar-kameez, stuck her glasses firmly on her nose and dragged herself to the Great Painful Family Dinner awaiting her.

* * *

Before leaving for work the next morning, Mini checked out of Pritam Pal's life. Her friend, Aditi, had been more than happy to have Mini as a paying guest. Bags packed, she waited for Rustom to arrive. But after last night's disaster, Mini had decided to go slow on the flirting. Also, she figured, she would have to shed some pounds before someone like Rustom gave her a second look. She was quiet on the way to the office, nodding as Rustom pointed out landmarks on the way.

The Mumbai office of Soul Mates was located in Andheri. How symbolic, Mini thought. Soul Mates in Andheri. Marriage in the Blind Alley! Very apt.

The lift took Mini and Rustom to the thirteenth floor. Another sign, thought Mini. Thirteen was her lucky number. Inside the office, things were pretty much like they were in the Delhi office, only more hectic. It seemed more people hired wedding planners in Mumbai. Mini noticed that preparations were being made for at least four weddings.

Rustom showed her to her cabin and disappeared down the hall. Mini was left to her own devices. She switched on the computer and checked her email. There were two bank statements, her mobile bill, her credit card payment reminder and an invitation to enroll for the 'Happy Family Insurance Scheme'. Mini forwarded all of them to Shyam. He was the one who looked after the financial stuff. She firmly deleted the 'Happy Family Insurance Scheme' offer. Right now, she was on a different mission and The Great Indian Family was not part of it.

A young woman came in and left a file on the table, with a note from Rustom to go through the contents. She introduced herself as Rustom's secretary, blushing as she spoke. Mini noticed that the man had most of the young girls in the office in a tizzy. But then, he was worth tizzying over, Mini sighed. He was tall, impeccably dressed, cologned and after-shaved, with an aquiline nose, strong jaw, intense eyes, flat stomach and thick, black hair. To top it all, he made a woman feel like she was the only one in the whole world. Mini determined that her first task in Mumbai would be to get Rustom into a tizzy.

She began to leaf through the file. So this was it, the no-budget-Mrinaliniji-no-budget wedding! She saw a picture of the groom. He was tall, dark and ... well ... you can't have everything. A Rajput prince, one of the few genuine ones left in the world, he was top pedigree. At twenty-four, he had graduated from Harvard in business management and returned to India a year ago. The prince was fond of racehorses and his doting daddy had gifted him a stud farm as a wedding present. A newspaper cutting showed the groom with his favourite horse – a black stallion of unmistakable breeding.

Some people get it all on a platter, Mini thought. There was nothing on the girl's background other than what Mini knew from the gossip columns. No mention of the bride's likes and dislikes, her favourite colours or outfits. Mini made a mental note to ask Rustom about the bride. As far as Mini knew, she was a rather slutty starlet with a few racy films to her name. She had suddenly shot into the limelight when the prince had proposed to her.

When was Prince Charming going to make an appearance in her own prosaic life, Mini found herself thinking. She forced her mind back to the file. Rumour had it that the prince himself was quite a stud, and that the bride was pregnant with his child. The honourable prince had decided to get married as his was a dying race and future studlings were to be preserved, even if it meant marrying a starlet.

* * *

That night, Mini and Aditi had their first heart-to-heart since Mini had arrived, sipping wine and demolishing chocolate-chip cookies. They talked of the other girls in the gang and caught up on children, dogs, parents and affairs. Mini wondered why sweet, pretty Aditi still didn't have a man in her life. Perhaps it was because of her parents' messy divorce. Or, maybe, she hadn't met Mr Right. As far as Mini knew, Aditi hadn't had a single serious relationship so far.

Aditi was very fond of Shyam, so Mini did not breathe a word about Rustom and her crush on him. Not that anything was going to happen. It was only a lark, but impending menopause had changed the rules of the game for Mini.

In any case, Aditi wouldn't understand. There was no way Mini could share with anyone the deep hunger she felt, the gnawing need inside her to meet a man who would fill her up so completely that she would be sated, needing no one and nothing else.

Looking down at the empty plate of cookies, Mini realized that she had eaten them all. Aditi had hardly touched them. Mini cursed herself. Why was it that, when it came to food, she didn't have a control button? She was a bottomless pit, an abyss. Any amount could be shovelled in and she would still want more. Disgusted, Mini decided to punish herself. Only fruit and water for the next three days, come what may, she promised herself.

In the morning, Aditi waved passes for a Sufi music concert under Mini's nose. Mini was unfamiliar with the genre but she decided to go along. It would be better than sitting in the flat alone and imagining ghosts behind curtains. They agreed to meet up after work and go for the concert together. Mini packed a skirt and a blouse in her bag for the evening. She also packed some of her newly acquired make-up and a pair of high-heeled shoes, just in case she met someone exciting.

★ ★ ★

A brainstorm session was scheduled in the conference room with the creative and production teams in attendance. Rustom, as branch head, was presiding. He made a brief presentation about the bridegroom and his family. They were the last living kings of their lineage and lived in a huge palace in Srirajmahalpur. The bridegroom was the heir apparent and was treated like a national treasure by his clan. He was the only son, though there were several sisters – each married to an erstwhile prince in turn. They would all be there for the wedding with their respective entourages – retinues of serfs, pets, masseurs, stylists, couturiers and astrologers. Rustom had it down to the last detail, even the names of the family's chief dogs, Raja William III and Rani Victoria IV.

Rustom then threw the discussion open. The usual clichés came up. A gold-and-silver discotheque wedding. A five-star-hotel wedding with well-known film stars as chefs. A truly absurd one was to have the wedding in a custom created ice-skating rink and have the guests skate in. An especially daft intern suggested that since this was going to be the ultimate grand wedding, it could be held in the Grand Resort.

'It's very grand, Sir,' he said, convincingly, among hoots of derision from the rest of the team.

Rustom brushed him aside. 'No, no. The Grand was used six months ago by the Singhanis. It won't do.'

Everyone was thinking hard, trying to come up with a winner of an idea. A little chit from Production piped up. 'Sir, I have an idea for the theme. How about using pink and mauve? Everything can be that colour ... it will look so pretty! And purple is a royal colour, right?'

Rustom snubbed her politely. 'Nice, but done last year, for the Bikhchandani couple's Valentine's Day party, remember?'

'I heard that the bridegroom is crazy about horses. Let's do something with horses,' another suggestion came up.

'But what? Everyone has a chariot these days,' piped the chit from Production.

Rustom kept looking at Mini, expectantly, waiting for her to share some spectacular ideas. Mini tried, but could think of nothing. Wishing she could catch the next flight to Delhi, she squirmed, trying to hide behind a tall potted plant, her palms breaking into sweat. One of the younger girls in the team spoke up. 'How about doing a submarine wedding? No one has done it so far in India!'

Rustom nodded encouragingly. 'Any more thoughts? Mini?' he asked, pointedly.

Mini looked up, now desperate, and said the first thing that occurred to her. 'You've told us so much about the bridegroom and his family, but what about the bride? Doesn't she have a say in this?' Nerves made Mini blabber on non-stop. 'Do you think women are like cows, kisi bhi khoonti say baandh do?'

'We've been hired by the groom,' Rustom interjected, hurriedly.

But Mini was too panicked to stop. 'Have you forgotten, this is the land of swayamvars!'

Rustom jumped up. 'Brilliant idea, Mini! A swayamvar! That's it! Superb!'

Mini was quick to recover lost ground. She continued talking, building on the idea before she lost her nerve. 'How about we arrange for the bride to be carried away on a horse? We will set up the wedding on the beach. And ... yes! The theme will be Runaway Bride! What do you think? After all, the prince is educated abroad. We can even print invites that say, "On 19 February, Prince Mangaji Sayaji Singhji is going to carry away Pinky Punjabi from under your nose! Be prepared or be surprised!" And we'll have all these horses – with tough riders – guarding the bride and groom, and they will all be holding ornamental swords ... it will be the talk of the town!'

The whole room was listening, rapt. The intern did an impromptu imitation of Mahatta. 'What an idea Mrinaliniji, what an idea!'

Rustom gave him a stern look. But the idea had caught everyone's imagination.

The young chit sighed wistfully. 'How romantic! I wish someone would sweep me off my feet like that.'

Mini was now on a roll. 'The bridegroom will be on a black charger. His will be the tallest horse, majestic, handsome, stately. When the bridegroom rides up, all other suitors will move away on their own, such will be his power!'

The young chit sighed again. 'Wow! It sounds like a dream!'

Mini elaborated still further. 'And the bride, she will be watching from the balcony. And as soon as she sees her Prince Charming, she will descend from a ladder of flowers, right on to the black horse and together they will ride into the sunset to live happily ever after.'

She noticed that Rustom was beaming from ear to ear. Encouraged, Mini let her imagination run away with her. 'Or we could try something else. We could have a line-up of male models, standing on the beach. The bride will come with a garland of red roses and pretend to choose her groom from among them. From the other direction, the bridegroom will gallop up on his stallion. He will scoop up the bride and carry her away. In the background, ethnic dancers will perform and folk singers will invoke the story of Samyukta and Prithviraj Chauhan.'

She stopped. The room had filled with deafening applause. Rustom spoke up. 'Let's make sure it all happens just the way Mini has described it. All right, back to work. Thank you, everyone.'

Rustom gazed at her with newfound respect. Their eyes met. Mini felt a shiver of anticipation down her spine. The man should come with a warning label, Mini thought. *Dangerous. Liable to make women swoon.*

Back in her cabin, Mini logged on to Google and typed 'Samyukta'. She had found a few interesting sites, when a chat-bubble popped up. It was Deepa from Delhi! Mini quickly typed a greeting.

Mini – 'Hello ☺'
Deepa – 'Hi! Howz Mum? Having fun?'
Mini – 'So far so gud.'
Deepa – 'Howz GP?'
Mini – 'GP hu?'
Deepa – 'Gay Parsi!'

Mini – 'He's all right. Very busy.'

Deepa – 'I heard something on the grapevine.'

Mini – 'What exactly?'

Deepa – 'He's a skirt-chaser.'

Mini – 'And I do wear skirts, sometimes.'

Deepa – 'Ha ha ha!'

Mini – 'Why, you don't think he'll go for me?'

Deepa – 'Are u serious? U R GOING 2 HAV AN AFR?'

Mini – 'Shhh. Don't tell anyone. I'm going to have an affair but not with GP.'

Deepa – 'Then who?'

Mini – 'Mahatta! Ha ha ha! K, gtg, c u, tc.'

Deepa – Ha ha ha! Bye, miss u, have fun!'

Deepa signed out and went back to Samyukta's story. The more she read, the more rapt she became. It was primitive, earthy, goosebumpy stuff. Mini played it on the screen in her brain as she read, her imagination amplifying it a thousand fold.

Samyukta's father, Raja Jaichand, and Prithviraj Chauhan were sworn enemies. When the king found out that Prithvi wanted to marry Samyukta, he came up with a novel idea. He would host a swayamvar. Every prince in the land received an invitation, even nonentities with kingdoms as tiny as mustard seeds. Except for Prithviraj Chauhan, the pretender to Delhi's throne. Instead, a mud statue was made in his likeness and placed at the entrance. Prithviraj was to be the gatekeeper at the swayamvar, derided and laughed at by all those who entered.

The day of the swayamvar dawned. Thundering hooves resounded in the air, the horses' manes shiny with sweat. Samyukta stood at the latticed window of her father's palace, her veil thrown back, peering anxiously at the growing gathering.

Would the man of her dreams appear and rescue her from her dreary existence? Then she saw him, astride a black horse, cantering at lightning speed. One great leap and the horse crossed over, into the palace. Samyukta entered the courtyard, holding a garland of flowers. She looked straight ahead, turning a deaf ear to the infatuated sighs of the suitors and a blind eye to their amorous stares. Her heart beating fast, she walked right past all the lovelorn suitors and draped the garland on Prithviraj's statue! Before Jaichand could react, Prithviraj appeared from behind the statue and, in one fell swoop, lifted Samyukta right off her feet.

Tears slid silently down Mini's chubby cheeks. Would Prince Charming appear in her own sorry life or would she have to wait till the next lifetime, she mused, morosely. What she would give to be Samyukta, for one lifetime, even for one measly day. Suddenly, she was famished. She was on a fruit diet, she remembered. But of their own volition, her hands reached into her bag and pulled out her emergency ration of chocolates.

Chomping pensively, she wondered if Rustom was going to be her knight-in-shining-armour. That reminded her; Rustom had still not provided any details about the bride-to-be. Without bothering to call, she trudged to his cabin, down the hall, and walked in without knocking. What she saw made her slam the door and run back to her cabin at top waddling speed. Rustom had had his arms around Sandra, his secretary. She had her head on his shoulder. Her skirt had ridden up from the back, revealing garters and pale, pink flesh with varicose veins.

Mini was still trying to recover from the shock when Rustom came in, looking dapper and as unruffled as ever. He sat down. An uncomfortable silence followed. Mini fidgeted with the keys of her computer, embarrassed and somewhat angry. Deep down, she wanted to be the one in Rustom's arms. But this man was sordid, going about seducing economically deprived secretaries. He was misusing his power and position.

Rustom broke the silence. 'Mini, it's not what you think. Sandra's father is in hospital and she just got a call ... it seems his condition is worsening. I was just ... consoling her.'

'Oh! I thought...' Mini piped up, thoroughly relieved.

'You don't know me very well, do you?' Rustom said. 'Actually, I don't know you either. What do you say we remedy that? Dinner tonight?' Rustom asked.

Mini's heart leapt up. 'Sure. Give me ten minutes to freshen up.'

She texted Aditi to cancel their evening plans and left for the ladies' room, glad that she had carried a change of clothes and shoes.

He took her to Rodeo Bar, one of the most exclusive dining places in the city. The staff greeted him like a regular and many people stopped by their table. The man was very suave, Mini noted. Feeling a little out of her depth, she let him do the ordering and discovered that he was an expert on wine and French cuisine. Mini thought of the last time she had gone out for dinner in Delhi with Sicko Shyam. He had taken her to Central Market and wolfed down several plates of chholey bhaturey, with chutney and grated mooli. Refusing dessert, he had rounded off the meal with a fizzy cola and then let out disgustingly smelly burps all evening.

Tonight was a sharp contrast. Soft music, cultured voices, gourmet food and an attentive companion. Mini sat back and let herself be seduced. If Shyam was like Old Monk, Rustom was like single malt, reflected Mini. Smooth. Urbane. Debonair. Sophisticated. Completely at home with the finer things of life.

Shyam was like a ball-scratching truck driver in comparison, thought Mini with derision.

As if on cue, her phone rang. It was Shyam. Mini quickly pressed the mute button and typed a text, telling him she was in a business meeting.

Rustom asked her about her family, the Delhi office, what she enjoyed most about her work. Mini found herself telling him things she normally would not share with a virtual stranger. But then, Rustom and she wouldn't be strangers for very long, she figured. They were going to be thrown together constantly as they worked on the biggest project Soul Mates had handled so far. She might as well start feeling comfortable with him so they could work efficiently. It was difficult, because his drop-dead-gorgeous-Greek-god looks kept coming in the way, making her painfully aware of him as a man.

Mini was too keyed up to eat much. Partly because Rustom was giving her delicious butterflies in the stomach and partly because Shyam had called incessantly, throughout the meal. Mini wondered what he wanted. If it was really urgent, he would have texted her, Mini knew. Shyam was extremely lazy when it came to texting; he didn't bother unless it was an emergency. In any case, the food was fashionably bland, no masalas at all. Which was perfect, thought Mini. She already seemed to have shed at least a kg since coming to Mumbai. But if she wanted Rustom to look at her, she would have to accelerate things. Mini made a mental memo to find out about gyms near Aditi's place.

She, in turn, quizzed Rustom about his life. He told her about his ancestral home in the suburbs, his wife who was wheelchair-bound and his son, who he had to look after. He told her how he often sat, late at night, with his son to do his school projects.

Mini's heart went out to Rustom. Life was universally bitchy, she thought. Scratch beneath the surface and everyone in the world had a sad story. Who would have guessed, looking at Rustom, how much suffering he carried within him? Mini longed to soothe the pain away with some tender loving care.

Rustom dropped Mini at Aditi's door, insisting on coming up and seeing her in safely. Aditi was in her nightclothes and scurried away after muttering a breathless 'hello' to Rustom. Saying goodbye, he gave her hand a tight squeeze. 'Thank you for coming to Mumbai, Mini. I'm really looking forward to us working together. See you tomorrow. Good night.'

Mini went to bed with a blissful smile on her face.

Next morning, when they were having their morning tea on the balcony, Aditi asked Mini about Rustom. 'Who was that sexy man who dropped you home last night? I want an intro!'

Mini pretended to be disinterested. 'Oh, him? That was Rustom, from the office. I'm working with him on that royal wedding project. And he's married.'

'Married? So what? You're married and that hasn't stopped you from thinking about other men, has it?' Aditi remarked, looking pointedly at Mini. Mini busied herself with stirring her tea, a tell-tale red patch on her cheeks.

'You thought I wouldn't notice? All these new clothes, make-up, the new contact lenses – it can mean only one thing. There's a new man in your life! Come on, fess up, Mini, you can tell me, we go back such a long way. Come, out with it!' Aditi probed away but Mini knew that anything she said would be relayed faithfully to all the other girls in their school gang and if Aditi thought there was real cause for worry, to Shyam as well. She laughed away Aditi's questions, telling her that her attempts to look good were just fear of aging.

Later, after Aditi had left for work, Mini wondered if she was even capable of having a relationship with a man other than Shyam. For one, would she be able to live a lie? Could she arrange secret trysts while pretending to be meeting the girls, send SMSes on the sly? Would she be able to go through with the deception, bear the constant strain of scheming and cheating? It was one thing to think about adultery, but to actually commit it? Mini was not sure she could. On the other hand, she argued, was it wrong for her to want a bit of romance if her marriage was not gratifying her needs? And what about sex? Her sex life had become non-existent lately. Did Shyam miss sex? If he did, he certainly wasn't showing any signs. Mini had a deep suspicion that early menopause was a withdrawal symptom of too little sex. Use it or lose it, isn't that what they said?

Her thoughts moved to Rustom. Could she do the male equivalent of slam-bam-thank-you-ma'am, sleep with him and walk away unscathed the next morning? Was she capable of sex for sex's sake? Deep down, Mini knew that sex alone would not satisfy her. She wanted the flowers, the violins, the valentines and the serenades. Rustom was so perfect. Just the thought of him made her knees buckle. God knows, she found him attractive enough. But no way was she going to rock the boat too hard. All she desired was a little interlude, a dream sequence. Then she would embrace reality with a secret smile and have the last laugh. It would all depend on whether she could seduce a man. *That* would depend on whether she could lose weight. And *that*, in turn, would depend on whether she could go to the gym regularly and if she could control her binge-eating. Well, this time she had strong incentive. Earlier, all her makeover attempts had been half-hearted stabs at Shyam's failing attraction towards her. This time, the prospects were far more rewarding. A last, hurrah, a true blue hot-blooded romance before menopause!

It was a cause worth dieting for.

* * *

Life fell into a set routine. Mini woke up early, trudged to the gym, came back for a quick shower and spent a good hour dressing for work. Her wardrobe had expanded and was now pretty strong on skirts. But she had a problem. Her weight was not coming down fast enough; she needed to have a talk with her gym instructor. After all, his claim to fame was the six-pack abs on several Bollywood hopefuls. Getting Mini down to size zero ought to be child's play.

The gym was in Aditi's building compound itself. This was just one of the many plus-points about Mumbai, Mini grudgingly acknowledged. In Delhi, distances and traffic snarls had kept her from joining a regular fitness programme. She concluded her morning's workout and stood hopefully on the weighing scales. The gym instructor was bent low, noting down the scale reading. Mini admired his neat, muscled bottom. The man could be a film star himself, with his toned body and well-defined chest. She had noticed how the teens and tweens in the gym tittered when he strutted past. If only he kept his mouth shut, because then the scales dropped from the eyes, as jat antecedents and gram pathshala accent came out of hiding.

Her weight hadn't moved a milligram. She accosted the instructor. 'Can we speed up the weight loss, boss?' she asked.

The gym instructor beamed reassuringly. 'Ma'am, muskle is haavier that weight. Your body is converting flab into sinew. Give it some time, then the weight will come down aatomatically, you'll see.'

Mini stood tight-lipped. Time was what she did not have. For one, menopause loomed darkly on the horizon. Secondly, she would soon have to return to Delhi. Rustom was not going to wait forever. 'What if I told you I've been offered a role in a movie? I need to be in shape, fast!'

Newfound respect dawned in the instructor's eyes. 'Oh! Why didn't you tale me before?' He sprinted away, disappearing behind a closed door. When he emerged, he had a big plastic tub in his hands. There were pictures of beefy men with bulging muscles printed on the label. 'This is a bawdy booshter. You take this, your body get muskle like Sunny Deol! Only three-thousand-two-hundred rupees, spacial discount price, only for you,' he said, triumphantly, as though he had come up with a solution to global warming.

Mini stared, speechless.

'Aapke arms, alraady like wrestler, vaary strawng! Only belly, very looj. You take this powder, you get muskles all over!'

Mini was aghast. How dare he call her a wrestler? So okay, her arms were a little thick, but that was the whole idea of joining a gym, for heaven's sake. She was waiting for the day she could wear sleeveless dresses and noodle straps. Now this beefy trainer wanted to add triceps to her biceps.

'I'm not looking for muscle, just weight loss,' she said, fixing him with a glare.

'But only weight laas, then waat you will do when skin becomes hanging? Aal wrinkled, like Rekha's? Then, only Buttocks!' he retorted back.

Mini stared. Then it dawned on her. He meant Botox. She gave up. Clearly, she was going to have to think of something else; this gym thing wasn't going to deliver. She walked back into Aditi's flat and was instantly swamped by the world's most heavenly aroma. Aditi was frying up cheese omelettes. She offered to whip up one for Mini. Mini felt herself melting, the way Samyukta would have when she set eyes on Prithviraj. The food devils and the diet angels started their battle.

Eggs are healthy and even dieters need a break now and then, the devils suggested silkily.

But what about her romantic dreams and her seduction plans, the angels argued.

The devils had many more arguments up their sleeves. She had just quit the gym, they reminded her. Before she got on to something more effective, she could live a little, couldn't she? For all she knew, the diet prescribed by the gym was even now converting her fat to muscle. She needed to take remedial action, right away. Involuntarily, Mini's hand reached out for a plate.

The diet angels retreated, knowing they were fighting a lost cause, but not without a parting shot. 'You will never be slim, Mrinalini. Your name should not be Mini, it should be Maxi Mehta,' they taunted. 'When you squirm your way into Rustom's arms, you will find they can't reach around you. Get ready for the extra seat belt in the aeroplane, fatso!' they jeered.

Mini ignored the angels and added a generous blob of butter to her toast. The omelette was heavenly and she ate it with undisguised lust. Ten minutes later, she was filled with self-loathing. She wasn't a woman, she was a mouth. A wide, open, gaping mouth. Always hungry, insatiable.

Upset with herself, Mini stirred extra sugar into her coffee cup. Why was she so helpless when it came to food? She had read on the web that, people who had no control over their eating were actually feeding other hungers. What void was she trying to fill, Mini asked herself. What would make her feel whole again? Whatever it was, food was *not* the answer, Mini told herself firmly, while her hand reached for an extra slice of cheese.

\* \* \*

Rustom had gone to make a preliminary presentation to the groom's family. Mini was on tenterhooks, itching to know the client's reaction to the swayamvar idea. She fervently hoped he would buy it. It was an idea close to her heart and Mini felt as nervous as Samyukta would have been.

Right on cue, her Prithviraj arrived. It was Rustom, looking pleased as punch. The client had loved the idea. He had given an unconditional go-ahead, in keeping with his unlimited budget. It was boom time at Soul Mates. Rustom was so thrilled, he pulled Mini out of her chair and did an impromptu waltz with her, making Mini's heart gallop like Prithviraj's horse.

The day was spent accepting congratulations from the rest of the office as people from the finance, creative and production departments poured in, shouting out 'Yippee!' and 'Party!' in alternate breaths. Even Mahatta called to offer congratulations. Deepa sent a long mail, extolling Sonal's seething jealousy. Mini was elated. It felt so good to have her work appreciated and her idea approved. Now she would do everything it took to ensure its perfect execution.

Rustom had asked for a meeting with her, to set deadlines and make a responsibility chart. Let him make all the charts and graphs he wants to, Mini thought. The actual work was done by the creative department, headed by her. Rustom and the production team were just the glorified errand boys, the ones who did all the running around. Just as well he had called for a meeting. She was going to make it clear that Soul Mates was a creative outfit and she was the creative boss. Period. She had to admit, though, that Rustom was good at what he did. He was non-interfering, efficient and organized. As long as he respected the creative team and left them alone, she was going to enjoy working with him.

Mini spent hours researching swayamvars with the design team, jotting down first thoughts on venue decor, menus, music, gifts, guest lists ... the to-do list was never-ending. Well, thought Mini, mentally rolling up her sleeves, it was time to show the amateurs how a professional handled things.

While things would heat up only in the last week before the wedding, there was a flurry of pre-wedding events to prepare for.

The bridegroom wanted to set the festivities rolling with a friendly polo match on his new stud farm. Soul Mates had been asked to organize the event. Rustom asked Mini to concentrate on the swayamvar, opting to manage the polo match with assistance from juniors in the team. But the prince's manager sent an invite exclusively for Rustom and Mini, summoning them to the event. He wanted them to approve the horses for the swayamvar.

Mini was secretly looking forward to the outing. Ever since Rustom had taken her out for dinner, she had been waiting for a chance to be alone with him. They were two, lonely people, cheated by fate into compromising their romantic agendas – he with his wheelchair-bound wife, she with Sicko Shyam. If Samyukta was one of her kindred spirits, Rustom was surely the other. Talking to him felt so right. Plus, the polo match was a great opportunity to show off her slightly slimmer self, in yet another newly acquired outfit which was dressy enough for the polo match but not too overdressed for office. Aditi and she had bought it together from an expensive designer boutique in Bandra.

'You should stick to fitted silhouettes and dark, basic colours, especially black,' the designer had advised. 'No fussy designs. Go for the semi-formal look, it will show off your curves, without making them conspicuous.'

Mini was not sure she understood the designer but when she tried on the mid-length black skirt, everything became clear. The material clung to her hips in such a flattering way, even Aditi paid her the ultimate compliment. 'You look sexy, Mini!'

She couldn't wait for Rustom to see her in it.

★ ★ ★

Mini had been deliberately ignoring Shyam's calls. The man thought he could call her whenever he wished to. He didn't seem to understand that she was a professional and couldn't be disturbed when in meetings or otherwise at work. Now he had actually taken the trouble of writing an email to her. Mini was rather pleased. She clicked it open with a sense of anticipation, but the feeling soon turned into irritation, followed by intense indignation.

'Mrinalini!!! How could you? You just upped and vanished, without a thought! How am I supposed to manage? I know you are a hot-shot working woman jet-setting around the country, but I don't care two hoots about that. As my wife, your first and foremost job is to look after me and take care of the house.

And you coolly flew off to Mumbai, without giving me the Wi-Fi password!!! My innumerable phone calls to find out the same, went unanswered. I must have called you at least a hundred times. What are you so busy with, may I ask? I have been unable to access the laptop or the desktop at home. And you know very well that this is peak cricket season. How am I to check on the test series being played in Australia? You also know that I have forgotten the Wi-Fi password many times before and that the home Wi-Fi passwords and such other things are your explicit responsibility. You do remember, don't you, that I start my day by checking the cricket scores, every morning? If I was the betting kind, I could have lost a fortune and that would serve you right.

Text or mail the Wi-Fi link immediately!!! I am inviting the boys to view the floodlit match tonight and I must, repeat, must, have access to the computers at home.

Be more careful in the future. Or else.

S.'

Mini seethed with rage. If long-distance looks could kill, Shyam would have vaporized by now. The gall of the man, Mini thought, flushed with anger. There was no way she was going to send the Wi-Fi password to him. He had a hope in hell, after that disgusting email. What a chauvinistic pig she was married to. Familiarity breeds contempt, was the popular phrase. But in her case, it was more like distance breeds pure hatred. Obviously, living with the man in such close proximity had blinded her to his horridness. Especially when she compared him with Rustom.

Mini hit the reply button and quickly dashed off a mail.

'Darling! How are you? I miss you so, so much. There is no one to snore me to sleep. I am so sorry you had to face inconvenience because of me. Here is the wretched password that I forgot to leave behind – ASSHOLE1. If that doesn't work, try this one – SICKOSHYAM1.

Enjoy the cricket with your batty friends.
Lots of love,
M'

\* \* \*

Mini couldn't wait to leave with Rustom for the polo match. But there was so many things demanding her immediate attention. Invitation designs had to be sent to the printer and Mini needed to finalize the colour scheme. Her table was crowded with paper samples in every hue and texture. What would royalty go for? Imperial maroon? Nah, too obvious, she thought. Black was an option. Nah, too funereal. Red? Been-there-done-that.

She opened a magazine lying on the desk. The cover story was titled 'The Flaming Bride'. Now that was an idea. Mini decided on saffron. That would be just the right touch of sophistication. She zeroed in on saffron-yellow handmade paper embedded with strands of real saffron. Saffron-yellow would be the theme colour and would be followed everywhere. Guest rooms would sport saffron-yellow curtains, saffron-yellow bedspreads, saffron-yellow serviettes, right down to the toilet paper.

Yellow toilet paper? Then again, maybe not, Mini figured. That would be a tad too much reality for the royals. Let it stay white. Going through the printer's colour guide, she tick-marked the exact Pantone shade of saffron-yellow she wanted. She was about to write a note to instruct that the toilet paper be kept white, when the phone rang.

It was Shyam. Mini grimaced. Was he going to crib about the Wi-Fi password, again?

'Shyam? I'm in a meeting, I'll call you back in the evening,' she said, trying to sound busy and indifferent, lest he get the impression that she was pining for him. Shyam's voice sounded suspiciously croaky. 'What's wrong, stayed up all night trying to guess the Wi-Fipassword?' she asked.

'Down with fever. Haven't slept … cancelled tonight's dinner,' he said, coughing. Years of habitual wifely concern struggled to fight its way out, and won.

'Is it your bronchitis? It's that time of year again. Call Dr Bhatt and get him to write a prescription, okay?'

'Can't you come back, Baby? I miss you,' pleaded Shyam.

Mini shook her head. Give an inch, take a yard, she thought. Who did he think she was, his nanny? 'Shyam, I'm here on work. And you're a grown man; stop behaving like you're two-years-old.'

Shyam sniveled loudly, desperately playing the sympathy card. 'But you've always looked after me! I need you to take my temperature and feed me soup,' he whined.

Mini was moved, but not very. 'Shyam, behave yourself. Call Dr Bhatt and start on a course of antibiotics. Bye.'

In the early days of their marriage, Mini had been devoted to Shyam. She had smothered him with attention. When he was ill, she had really suffered.

She remembered watching a movie about a dog called Hachiko. It was a true story. Every day, come rain or sunshine, the dog would be at the station to receive his master when he returned from work. One day, the master died of a sudden heart attack. The dog continued to wait every day at the station. The world moved on, the professor's family shifted residence, but Hachiko would arrive sharp at 5.00 p.m. and stand vigil, awaiting his master's return. Mini was thoroughly overcome by this shining example of love and loyalty. She told Shyam that she would be his Hachiko, pledging to be as faithful as a dog. Mutt-crazy Shyam thought it was the best compliment she could have paid their relationship. For months after that, he called her Hachi mere Saathi. Those were the days, Mini sighed. Soon after, Mini started calling Shyam 'mad dog', while he dubbed her 'crazy canine' – his euphemism for 'bitch'.

The daft intern was waiting at the door, wanting to know the Pantone shade to be ordered. Mini handed him the guide and asked him to add the note about keeping the toilet paper white. Her mind was still on Shyam. Men! They wanted a mother, not a wife … romance be damned! She could bet a million bucks that Shyam wasn't really ill; he was just pretending, so that she would come back home and take care of things like always. Well, she wasn't budging, not this time, Mini resolved.

Sandra buzzed her at 3.00 p.m. on the dot; it was time to leave for the polo match. Mini eagerly picked up her handbag and dashed to the lift. The car stood at the building entrance, the rear door open. Mini slid inside and turned eagerly towards Rustom. He wasn't there. Instead, chewing on a piece of gum, there sat the daft intern.

'Where's Rustom?' she blurted out.

'He is busy, Ma'am. He has deputed me to escort you to the match,' the intern replied.

Deflated. That was how Mini felt. And cheated. Didn't Rustom want to be with her, she wondered despondently. Now she would be lumped with a silly intern for the evening. Feigning a headache, Mini closed her eyes, sudden tears prickling the back of her eyelids. Mumbai felt cold and uninviting. She wished she was back home in Delhi.

\* \* \*

The stud farm was on the Pune highway. The car cruised into a graceful driveway lined with tall trees on both sides. Mini pulled herself together. Stop being a baby, she reprimanded herself. She was going to enjoy the polo match, maybe even snag a prince or two!

The match was in full swing. The prince's friends and family sat in a canopied spectator area, sipping their daiquiris. Mini and the daft intern took their places with the rest of the hoi polloi. She looked around and her heart sank. She was completely out of place. The royal ladies were present in full force, in their French chiffons and Belgian diamonds. Rustom would have fit right in, with his imported suits and clipped accent. But she herself felt like something the cat dragged in. The daft intern looked like a peon. When the waiter hovered over her with a tray of drinks, she picked up two beers and gulped them in quick succession, closely followed by another three. Life began to look rosier. Even the daft intern started to look sweet. Her bladder, however, was ready to burst. The need of the hour was the loo. Urgently.

Mini tottered out of the pavilion, clutching her bag, trying to walk straight. Behind her, a constipated voice on the microphone announced the final chukkar of the match. Rustom was a bloody chhakka, that's what he was. Mini giggled at the thought. She was not going to think about the gay Parsi, she was not, she chanted to herself as she sank onto the toilet seat with a feeling of extreme relief. She was going to hold herself up with dignity.

*Pachak!* The severely tested, over-extended elastic band of her skirt snapped.

Now what, thought Mini, in a panic. How was she going to leave the loo? She got up. The skirt slid down, bunching around her knees. Could she go out in just her blouse? But her legs were not waxed above the knee. Mini gave up the idea. What else, she thought, wracking her brain. Should she call Aditi and have her deliver another skirt? No, that would take too long. Besides, she might pick out the wrong one. If only she had a piece of string, thought Mini, she could fashion a naara.

She looked around the loo. The towels were too thick to push through the waist band. She remembered the daft intern and called him from her mobile.

'Hello, Ma'am, where are you? The match is over and...'

Mini cut him short. 'Never mind the match! We have a crisis situation here. Can you find me a piece of string ... you know ... a naara? Or do you have a belt?'

'No Ma'am. Why? Can't this wait? The stud farm manager is waiting to take us to the stables,' he exclaimed.

Mini hung up on him. No help, these young trainees. They don't want to work hard, they just want to be spoon-fed, Mini tut-tutted. Why couldn't the idiot be resourceful, instead of asking useless questions? Anyway, she would have to think of something fast.

Mini rummaged through her bag. Nothing useful there ... lipstick, perfume, liner, condoms (you never know) and her phone charger. Phone charger! That was it! Feeling smug and very smart, Mini threaded the phone charger's wire into the waistband. It was perfect. And stronger than elastic. She tied a knot, tucked in the plug and walked out of the loo, secure and confident.

The daft intern was waiting alone in the now empty pavilion. As soon as he saw her, he began to walk towards the car, where the manager was waiting. They drove in silence to the stables located behind the polo ground. The manager explained that the prince would ride into the swayamvar on his favourite Arab stallion. What Mini was being shown were the lesser breeds. She looked at the horses. The brown ones looked the friendliest, the white ones were beautiful, while the black ones looked angry and dangerous. Mini told the manager to pick out a dozen white mounts, all of the same height, and have them ready for the day of the swayamwar.

She enquired about the prince's mount and the manager led her to a special enclosure. It was a brute of a horse. Tall, dark and handsome, that was the only way to describe him, Mini marvelled. If only they made men this way, she thought, thinking of pot-bellied Shyam. Rustom came close, though. But she was not going to think about Rustom any more, not after the way he had ditched her clean today.

Sensing strangers in his midst, the stallion snorted loudly. Unnerved, Mini quickly moved away and found herself next to the enclosure of a sweet, dappled grey pony. He reminded her of Polka. She reached out to stroke his head, crooning to him the way she had seen Chris Cooper do in *Seabiscuit*. Had she been Samyukta, she would have insisted on ponies for her swayamvar, she thought. They were so lovable, like oversized puppies. But this particular pony was a bit over-friendly; he was trying to sniff at her crotch!

Mini pulled away. And felt herself coming apart. The pony had her charger plug in his mouth and was tugging.

'Shoo boy! Down! Let go!' Mini whispered, frantically, holding on to her skirt for dear life. But the pony had no intention of letting go. She yelled loudly and the daft intern and the manager came charging. The manager pulled the charger out of the pony's mouth. Luckily, the cord had withstood the assault. He gave Mini a strange look. Mini gathered the shreds of her charger and tottered out, teetering on the edges of self-pity.

On the way back to town, the daft intern kept trying to control recurrent bursts of giggles. Mini pretended to talk to choreographers and designers on her mobile, giving him the royal ignore. Ungrateful creep, she thought. Here he was, rubbing shoulders with royalty, just because of her, and he had the gall to laugh at her! She had a good mind to have him sacked.

Over dinner at Aditi's that night, Mini told her about her visit to the stud farm. Aditi laughed so hard, Mini had to thump her back and wipe her tears. But she did offer some concrete suggestions for weight loss. A personal dietician could do the trick. She also suggested the use of corsets. Apparently, these magical things could keep all your fat out of sight. Mini was intrigued. She remembered reading about corsets and stays in old, English romances. The heroine always had to wear one, so that her waist would never measure more than eighteen inches. On her own body, eighteen inches would be the measure of one thunder thigh, Mini reflected. She decided to invest in corsets immediately – not just for her waist, but for her thighs as well.

# 3

---

Mini was mulling over design ideas for the wrapping paper, when a young dolt from Finance knocked on her cabin door. 'Ma'am, can I borrow your charger?' he asked. Mini looked up blankly and thrust her hand into her bag. Then she remembered. Her charger had been chewed.

'Sorry, I don't have one,' she said. The dolt ran off, smiling stupidly.

Ten minutes later, there was another knock. This time it was a giddy young art director from the creative department. 'Ma'am, do you do you have a charger? Please may I borrow it?' she asked.

'Sorry, I didn't bring my charger today,' She replied. The girl scurried away, grinning from cheek to cheek.

Mini went back to ruminating over wrapping paper. She had a brainwave. Return-gifts for the wedding would come wrapped in saffron paper with a miniature sword attached. To open the gift, one would have to slash through the wrapping with the sword. A lovely little royal touch, Mini thought, feeling smug. No wonder the youngsters in the office worshipped her. Like the young art director who had just come to borrow the charger. She had a lot to learn and Mini could teach her, if she had the right attitude and showed respect.

The intercom buzzed. It was Sandra. 'Ma'am, may I borrow your charger?' she asked.

What was it about chargers today? Mini thought, exasperated. It seemed the whole office had forgotten to bring theirs.

'Sorry, I don't have one,' she replied, going back to her computer.

She was looking up images of little scabbards on Google when, from the corner of her eye, she saw Rustom coming towards her cabin. Mini pretended to be deep in work, not looking up even when he came and stood behind her chair.

'Mini,' he said, clearing his throat. 'Er ... may I borrow your charger?' Mini stared at him, suspiciously. This was too much. Now Rustom also wanted her charger.

Then it dawned on her. The daft intern had told everyone about how her charger had been eaten by the pony! And Rustom, of all people, was in the joke! This was unbearable, Mini decided. She picked up a book and flung it at Rustom, following it up with a cushion. She was about to fling a heavy paperweight when Rustom caught her wrist and pulled her towards him. 'Easy, Mini, easy! I'm sorry, okay? I didn't mean to upset you. Nobody in the office will mention the charger again. Truce?'

Mini thawed a little. 'On one condition,' she said, as she took in the heady fumes of cigar smoke and cologne. 'We need some time together. I have to share my thoughts on several things. You have no time during office hours so you can buy me dinner.'

'Sure, whenever you like,' Rustom let go of her arm. 'Just tell me one thing, why did you tie your phone charger around your waist?' Mini looked around for something to fling. Rustom walked out of the room backwards, laughing non-stop as he shielded himself with his arms.

Mini swore vengeance. The daft intern would have to pay for

this. She would show him, Mini determined. Still, Rustom had almost held her, so close that she could see the sprightly hair on his chest. That was something to think about.

Work kept both Rustom and Mini busy. Mini was engulfed by endless discussions on backdrops, props, music, dance troupes, guest lists. There were bookings to be made, appointments to be fixed and the trousseau to be packed. But for Mini, the biggest concerns were the location of the swayamwar and the choreography. She would have to get just the right choreographer; she didn't want a Bollywood act turning the ceremony into a cheap spectacle.

She went through the list that Production had provided. So many of the choreographers were male. What did men know about weddings and decor? Unless of course, they were gay. Gay men made excellent choreographers, she knew from experience. But then, Rustom was in the wedding business and he was as male as they came. Unless he was a closet gay? Where would that leave her, stuck between a Neanderthal husband and a gay love interest, Mini reflected glumly.

She was jumping the gun, Mini reminded herself. As things stood, there was nothing between Rustom and her, but anything was possible. She had to be patient.

'Don't push it, don't force it. Let it happen naturally. It will surely happen, if love was meant to be.' The lyrics of a popular oldie popped up in her mind. The only problem was, she was on a deadline here. This was her last chance at finding Dream Lover. It was now or never.

Mini went back to pondering over locations. She had poured over the layouts of every luxury location in town. Nothing ready-made worked for the swayamvar setting. After much deliberation, Mini decided it would have to be a set. Maybe she should do a reconnaissance trip. Rustom would have to come along to figure out the feasibility. The coming weekend would be a good time.

Picking up the phone, she punched Rustom's extension. Sandra answered, saying that Rustom was in a conference call and would get back to her the moment his call ended. The girl practically lived in Rustom's cabin. Mini experienced a blinding flash of jealousy. Did Rustom have his arms around Sandra, like the time he had when she had barged in on them? She gave herself a mental shake-up. She would have to stop behaving like a besotted teenie bopper. She didn't want a roll in the hay or a mere one-night stand. She was looking for a soulmate, nothing less. Someone who would plug the hole in her heart. And if Rustom was the one, she would know. Just the way Julia Roberts had known in *Pretty Woman*, or Meg Ryan had, in *When Harry Met Sally*.

Rustom came on the line. Mini adopted her most professional tone and requested for the reconnaissance trip to be arranged. Was that Sandra giggling in the background? Mini's hackles rose. No way could Rustom be her Dream Lover. She was crazy to even consider him. Anybody who went for Sandra had to have exceptionally poor taste. She was better off without him, Mini decided.

Then why was a little voice telling her that grapes are sour?

\* \* \*

An entire week had gone by and Rustom had made no move towards the promised dinner. Mini tried to believe she couldn't care less. If work was suffering, it wasn't her problem alone. In fact, she had zeroed in on a choreographer and Rustom didn't even know. He hadn't replied to any of her emails.

After a lot of mulling and pondering, Mini had finally chosen Dancing Diva for the swayamvar choreography. They were not the best known choreographers in the city, but their portfolio suggested flamboyance and originality. Mini decided to go with her gut-feeling. She would have to work closely with them, lest they go over the top. Now the chief choreographer had requested for a meeting. His studio was in town, a long drive away from the Soul Mates office.

Since much of the swayamvar's success depended on the choreography, Mini insisted that Rustom accompany her to the meeting.

Rustom was unusually quiet as the two of them crawled through Mumbai's infuriating traffic. Mini kept to herself, typing notes and setting reminders on her phone. Choreographers were critical to any wedding, and especially so for this one. Every step the bride took had to be pre-planned. Then there were dances for all other ceremonies as well, like the mehendi ceremony. The mehendi artist had to be finalized urgently too, Mini thought as Rustom drove. Green Designs seemed promising but Henna Gehna was more interesting; their artists could ink the bridegroom's initials on the bride's palms in several languages, including Tibetan and Yiddish.

Mini thought back to her own wedding. According to Sicko Shyam, mehendi looked like gobar and made him sick. Mini sighed. Back then, she had found him so endearing and unique. Now she knew better.

At the studio, she went over the concept of the swayamvar in detail with the choreographer, showing him pictures of Samyukta and Prithviraj on Google Images. The choreographer was entranced while Rustom looked distinctly disinterested. What could be eating him, Mini wondered.

The meeting went off rather well. Mini was delighted by the ideas the choreographer threw up. With just a few movements and expressions, he had accurately captured the very essence of Samyukta. Mrinalini could visualize a fantastic show. She stepped out of the studio with a dance in her step.

'Congratulations Mr Rustom Mistry, we have stumbled upon a hugely talented choreographer!' she exulted.

She was met by gloomy silence. Rustom stopped the car abruptly by the kerb and sat gazing morosely at the sea.

Mini was alarmed. She touched him on the elbow. 'What's wrong, Rustom? Is something bothering you?' she queried.

He grimaced. 'Nothing. Nothing at all. Just a quarrel with the missus,' he muttered. Mini waited expectantly for more information. 'You are married, so you know, how small misunderstandings can lead to major problems,' Rustom said, looking at her wearily.

He looked so vulnerable, Mini wanted to reach out and smooth his handsome, creased brow. She nodded. 'You bet. My husband and I are always scrapping. So what happened?' Mini prodded.

Rustom heaved a huge sigh. 'I haven't done anything wrong, believe me. Ever since my wife had that bad accident, she's so crabby and suspicious, she thinks I'm having an affair with Sandra!' Rustom exclaimed.

Of course you are, Mini almost said, but caught herself in time. 'Want to talk about it? Come, let's take a walk,' she said instead, opening the door and walking towards the beach along the road.

Rustom locked the car and followed. They walked in

companionable silence for a while. Mini asked him why his wife was in a wheelchair.

'She was in a road accident a couple of months ago. Broke her hip bone. It's healing, but meanwhile she is confined to the house. Every time I'm working late, she calls up the guard to find out who else is in the office. I'm really fed up!' Rustom complained.

'But I work late as often as you do. I hope she doesn't suspect anything between the two of us?' Mini asked.

'On no, she would never suspect you! I've never looked at you in that way...' Rustom replied, quickly.

Mini was mortally offended. So Rustom didn't think he could have an affair with her. And she was considering him as a soulmate candidate. On the brighter side, at least the man was confiding in her. That was a start. With a warm and sympathetic smile on her face, she turned to Rustom and squeezed his arm reassuringly.

'Why worry so much? Your conscience is clear, that's the most important thing. Your wife will come round, you'll see. She will soon realize that she's just being silly. I mean, I know ... and not just me ... the whole office knows, you are just protective of Sandra because she is going through a difficult patch.'

Rustom turned to Mini, relieved. 'Thanks Mini, for believing in me ... you are such a wonderful person.'

They linked arms and walked back to the car. Inside, Mini was still a bit peeved. What did Rustom think of her? Was he even aware of her as a woman? Well, she was going to change all that, Mini swore. She would lose so much weight, Rustom would forget all about his wife, Sandra and every other woman on the planet.

★ ★ ★

Ever since Mini had arrived in Mumbai, the gang from school had been trying to meet up. Now one of the girls, Neelu Parikh, had invited them all to her place for dinner. After much ado and a lot of back and forth, the gang finally decided to go. She would get to meet almost everyone, Mini figured, looking forward to the madness and fun.

Neelu never was and never could be a bona fide member of the old girls gang. She was more of a hanger-on. There was a reason for that. She was a day scholar. There was an unwritten rule that day-skis – slang for day scholars – and boarders, did not mix. Mini recalled how Neelu had constantly curried favour with the boarders. She so desperately wanted to belong. They, on the other hand, had exploited her shamelessly. They ate her home-made tiffin every day, made her buy them ice cream at the tuck shop and bullied her into bringing all kinds of delicacies for them from home. The more Neelu tried to ingratiate herself with the gang, the more mean and wicked they became.

Mini wondered what Neelu would serve for dinner. She still remembered the taste of her mother's superb keema-matar. It was mind-blowing – cooked to perfection, replete with pure ghee and home-ground spices. It was one of those life-altering experiences that never quite leave you. She was already drooling in anticipation. Then she remembered. She had taken a mental vow to become the thinnest woman in her purview. There was no way she could eat that keema-matar. She would settle for a spoonful or two, just to check if the taste matched her memory of it.

Bhavna was picking them up. Aditi and Mini were bathed, perfumed and suitably attired. It was important to look good for these hen nights. The old girls were all in some sort of unacknowledged competition. Who had greyed more, who had put on weight (that would be me, Mini thought), who had gone under the surgeon's knife, who was divorced, who was still single. But none of them were bitchy or overtly critical. Once the initial exclamations were done with, the meetings invariably turned into reminiscences. They never tired of the same stories, of midnight feasts, mass bunks and secret crushes on the only male teacher on campus.

A peremptory honk announced a chauffeur-driven coupé and Bhavna's coiffure-end hair emerged. Aditi and Mini made a thoroughly undignified dash towards the car, where a cloud of expensive perfume and loud shrieks enveloped them. Hugs and kisses were exchanged. Snorts and giggles followed. The car moved swiftly towards Neelu's place. Mini felt more relaxed than she had felt in weeks. They could be meeting after years, but it did not matter in the least. They were as comfortable in each other's company today as they had been in the school dormitory all those years ago.

Mini looked forward to the evening. There was so much catching up to do. And there was Neelu's leg to be pulled, she thought gleefully.

They were let through a formidable gate by a walkie-talkie-wielding guard. A liveried butler showed them into a palatial drawing room. Scented candles wafted fragrance all around and a small water body gurgled near an open verandah. What kind of person owned such a place, that too in Mumbai? The girls exchanged glances. Who had Neelu married, a sheikh?

Surekha was the next one to arrive, the Ms Goody-Two-Shoes of the gang. She was the quintessential homemaker, attending kitchen-garden meetings and PTA sessions. Her other passion was collecting rocks – the shiny kind. Accompanying her was Dhira, Mini's favourite after Aditi. Dheeru bhai, as they had named her in school, was a social worker, probably the only one that the elite boarding school had produced since its inception.

They made a curious bunch, so different yet so comfortable in each other's company. It came from being thrown together for years in boarding school. After you had lived with a person for ten years in a row, familiarity, at least in this case, was a happy side effect.

A beautiful woman entered the room, tall, elegant, bejewelled, every inch reeking of grooming and wealth. Nobody moved. Then the vision let out a loud whoop and raced towards them, arms gracefully extended. Mini baulked. This was Neelu? Whatever had happened to the awkward thing in the torn uniform, with ink stains down the shirt front?

It took a few drinks for the ice to break and soon it was just like old times. Everyone wanted to know everything about everyone else. It was Neelu's turn first. When, how and to whom had she got married?

Neelu breezily told them how she had been swept off her feet by her husband, a hot-shot industrialist, soon after college. The man had spotted her buying stuffed teddy bears in a store and fallen head over heels in love. The very next day, a carload of teddy bears had arrived at her home, with a note from the gentleman, requesting a meeting. He was good-looking, extremely rich, with an impeccable family background. They were married in no time and were living happily ever after. Two cherubic children were ensconced in elite boarding schools in England. Neelu spent summers with them and winters in some Swiss ski resort or the other.

Mini could feel her self-esteem slide down her backbone and right down to her toes. Even funny old Neelu had done well for herself. She had a good-looking, rich, powerful man who worshipped the ground she walked on. What more could a woman want, Mini thought enviously.

Neelu's story settled on Mini like a pall of gloom. Try as she did, she couldn't shake it off. She should be happy for Neelu, she told herself, but there was no escaping the self pity that swamped her. When it was her turn to give a lowdown on her life, she tried to make it sound glamorous and exciting. She told the girls all about the royal wedding she was working on and fibbed that she was a partner in Soul Mates. There were murmurs of appreciation from everyone. Mini perked up. Then Neelu said that she knew the family and had already been sent a handwritten invitation on the prince's personal stationery.

Mini's bubble burst. She couldn't wait for the evening to end. Even three helpings of the keema-matar that Neelu had cooked especially for her, couldn't cheer her up. Instead, she drank glass after glass of imported diet beer and ended up standing in the middle of the fountain in the verandah, singing the school song at the top of her voice.

★ ★ ★

Next morning, the hangover didn't help. It only served to remind her that she would have to starve for a few weeks to make up for the extra calories. Diet beer was yet another of life's oxymorons; a minute on the lips and forever on the hips, Mini thought ruefully.

The office was dull. Rustom was away for the entire day, meeting caterers, and Mini was in a strange, restless mood, not up to tackling too much. She was hung-over, maudlin and fuzzy. She ambled about the office, desultorily checking invitation card graphics, peeking into people's work and catching up with Deepa on Google Chat. She glanced into Rustom's cabin. Sandra was seated at his desk, looking busy for a change.

Mini peeped at the computer screen. 'What are you doing, Sandra?' she asked.

'Rustom Sir said to take prints of Australian animals,' she replied reluctantly.

'Whatever for?' asked Mini, curious. 'What do Australian animals have to do with the royal wedding?' Mini was most bewildered. Maybe Rustom was planning a pet parade as part of the entertainment?

'Zubin, Rustom Sir's son, has to make a chart for school,' Sandra answered.

Aha! So this was how Rustom got his son's homework done, Mini thought. She was most discomfited. Why did Rustom lie to her, spinning tales about sleepless nights and a wheelchair wife? Surely he didn't need to fib for such a small matter. Mini tried to extract more information from Sandra but the woman clammed up like a sphinx. After a while, Mini started going batty, staring at pictures of the emu, cassowary and the duck-billed platypus. She sauntered back to her own cabin.

The homework issue got Mini all worked up. There was so much work pending but Mini couldn't concentrate. She played Spider Solitaire, losing game after game. The rest of the office was also in some sort of stupor. Soul Mates was going through a collective hangover, it seemed.

She was toying with the idea of leaving early for the day when the young visualizer from the art department walked into the cabin. She closed the door and sat down, a conspiratorial look on her face. What was up, Mini wondered.

The visualizer leaned forward and whispered. 'Ma'am, we

are playing a practical joke on Shox!' Shox was the daft intern who had accompanied Mini to the Polo match.

'Really? What exactly do you have in mind?' Mini enquired desultorily. The girl lowered her voice to a whisper and proceeded to outline the charade.

It was a diabolical plan. Mini looked at the visualizer with new respect.

'Very inventive, I must say. Now if you could put even half of that creativity into your designs, you would be a sensation…' she teased. The girl grinned sheepishly. 'So…why are you telling me all this? If you are worried I'll sneak on you, rest assured, mum's the word. In any case, I'm planning to leave early, so…' Mini said.

The girl twisted the ends of her hair nervously. 'Actually Ma'am, we were wondering if you could help us a little … I mean … if you were the one who handed over the 'task' to Shox, then he would be completely convinced,' she said.

Mini considered the request. She didn't care much for the daft intern, but on the other hand, a person of her rank and seniority couldn't be seen participating in petty pranks. Rustom wouldn't take it kindly.

'Look, I promise I'll look the other way, but keep me out of this, I'm not going to be a part of such childish office shenanigans. Now if you'll excuse me, I've got work to finish,' Mini said, dismissing the girl with a wave of her hand.

The girl didn't budge. 'Ma'am, honestly speaking, I didn't like it at all when Shox made so much fun of your charger. I thought it was so awful of him. I mean, why did he have to tell the whole office, especially Rustom Sir? I don't know how you can be so tolerant, Ma'am. If I were you, I would teach him a lesson!'

Mini remembered only too well. Her brow darkened. 'Okay, I'll help you,' she said tersely. 'You can call Shox to my cabin and tell him whatever you like, I'll just be there ... as a spectator, that's all. I am definitely not going to join in. Is that clear?'

The visualizer nodded, barely able to contain her excitement. 'Thanks, Ma'am, thank you so much! I'll get Sandra to do the talking. Your presence itself will be enough!' She skipped out, bursting to tell her co-conspirators.

After lunch, Sandra and Shox entered Mini's cabin. 'Close the door and sit down,' Mini said, schooling her features into a business-like demeanour.

'Ma'am, Rustom Sir must have called you ... he told me you will brief Shox,' Sandra said, poker-faced.

Mini pretended to be busy. 'I'm rather busy. You go ahead and brief him, Sandra,' she muttered, without taking her eyes off her computer screen.

Sandra cleared her throat. 'Rustom Sir has asked me to entrust a critical job to you. It's a very important task so he said to ask only you,' Sandra continued. Mini covertly watched the intern's face. Boy, does he look chuffed up, she thought.

'It's like this. The prince's maternal uncle is coming into town on the 4.00 p.m. flight. Problem is, he is a bit ... off.'

'Off?' echoed the daft intern. 'You mean he's a nutcase?'

'No no, just mildly crazy. You see, he still believes that he is a king,' Sandra clarified.

'So what do I have to do?' the daft intern asked.

'Nothing much. Just get hold of a royal retainer's costume. You have to wear it and go to the airport. When the gentleman arrives, just pretend that he is the king, escort him to his car and drop him to his hotel. That's all,' Sandra finished.

Mini swallowed a chuckle.

The intern looked quite wary. 'But how will I recognize him?' he asked. Sandra glanced at the clutter on Mini's table.

The previous day, Mini had been downloading pictures of royal costumes. Some printouts were still lying round. Sandra picked up one of a man in a gold-embroidered achkan with a matching turban and silently handed it to the daft intern.

Leaning forward, she addressed him with full gravitas. 'Now remember, this is a secret mission,' she said. 'The prince would be furious if news of his uncle's mental state got out. Not a word to anyone.'

The intern nodded, eyes wide. He marched out of the room, Sandra following closely behind.

Mini pictured the scene and was tickled pink. The daft intern would stand at the airport in full costume, playing retainer to imagined royalty. It was a priceless prank.

Shox was a suitling, a stuffed shirt in the making. Mini hoped that the prank would take some stuffing out of him. She remembered how he had behaved at the polo match. His crisis-management skills were abysmal, Mini recalled. All she had asked him to do was find a string. He couldn't even do something that simple. Had she been in his place, she would have immediately offered her tie. But suits didn't have the ability to think on their feet. They needed a PowerPoint presentation even to execute a sneeze. Mini shook her head silently as she lost yet another game of Solitaire. Shox's was a hopeless case, absolutely irredeemable. One more young life lost to suitdom, Mini thought idly.

The young visualizer had kept the office phone book open on the page that had Maganlal Dresswala's numbers. Shox fell for the bait. He dialled the number, whispering into the phone as he described the dress he was looking for. She watched silently as the courier boy from Maganlal Dresswala arrived. When Shox grabbed the package and ran towards the restroom, the young visualizer and Sandra exchanged high fives and danced with glee.

An hour later, Shox was as ready as he could be. The headgear was proving to be a bit of a challenge. It was loose and kept slipping down to his forehead and over his eyes, blinding him every now and then. He was preening in front of the mirror when Bala, from the accounts department, barged in. He had been banging on the bathroom door for a good while and was on the verge of calling the building guards. When he saw Shox in his finery, he exploded. 'What you are doing man, hogging the loo?' he demanded to know.

Shox smiled slyly. 'Sorry, can't tell you, it's a secret mission for the boss. Please don't tell anyone you saw me like this, okay?'

Bala's bladder was about to burst. He gave Shox a dirty look and slammed the door.

The office grapevine was abuzz. Shox was the hot topic of discussion. Everyone was burning with curiosity after Bala from Accounts had told them he had seen Shox in the toilet, wearing Ram Lila clothes. Several explanations were offered but none were thoroughly convincing. The young visualizer couldn't hold on to the secret. She told Bala who told the Admin chaps who told the dudes in Production and soon everyone in the office knew.

From being a private joke involving the daft intern and the creative team, the prank became office property. Now the stakes were higher.

Bala said he was sure that Shox would run back, he simply didn't have it in him to enact the role. The young visualizer disagreed. Shox would do anything to earn brownie points, she declared. An argument ensued. People took sides. Bala said he would shave his beard if Shox completed the task. The young visualizer said she would kiss Shox if he didn't. Mini turned a blind eye to the proceedings. Picking up her bag, she decided to go downstairs and visit a boutique round the corner. She needed retail therapy.

She emerged from the building to see a strange sight. Shox stood on the kerb in all his finery, trying to hail a cab. There were plenty cruising down the road but none stopped. Meanwhile, he was attracting a lot of attention. A prostitute standing across the road was giving him the once-over. As Mini looked on, the prostitute began to cross the road and walk towards him. Shox looked terrified. Mini actually felt sorry for him. She was about to blow the whistle on the prank when the prostitute let out a loud, ear-splitting one, the kind where you put two fingers in your mouth. Instantly, a taxi came to a halt right in front of Shox. He darted in and disappeared.

What an ungrateful person, Mini thought. He hadn't even thanked the prostitute. The man deserved what he was about to get. He needed to be pulled down a peg or two, she decided.

Mini knew that the rest of the office was going to the airport to see Shox in action. She had signed the permission slip. The young visualizer was even going to film the scene for posterity. They would be away for an hour at least, Mini figured. Enough time for her to go shopping.

Retail therapy proved to be rather painful that day. The boutique had nothing in her size. To add insult to injury, the starved kid who was masquerading as the salesgirl, told her that they didn't cater to 'mature women'. Basically, fumed Mini, their dresses were for Barbie dolls, not for real women. Barbie dolls were plastic; they didn't need elastic.

Back in office, she looked up 'Barbie' on Google. She was vindicated when she discovered that Barbie was unreal. That is, if Barbie was a real person, she would be six feet tall, weigh a mere hundred pounds and her vital statistics would be 39-21-

33. Also, she would not be able to hold her neck up and would have to crawl on all fours to get around. And to top it all, she would have severe medical problems. Engrossed in defaming Barbie on her social network, Mini forgot about Shox and the prank, till the visualizer arrived with the handycam and played the footage for her.

It was a hoot. The scene had clearly been shot from behind a pillar, the lens focusing on Shox who was silently memorizing the nonsensical lines from a piece of paper that the young visualizer had given him. 'Mughal-e-azam! Shehenshah! Badshah! Mumbai mein tashreef laaney ke liye shukriya. Ayiye! Padhaariye! Aapka sipaahi aapko uthaaney aaya hai!'

Shox's strange appearance had caused quite a stir. A group of camera-happy Japanese tourists stopped to take pictures, blocking the way. Passengers cursed. A buxom lady deliberately bumped Shox with her trolley, yelling 'Shoo! Shoo!' at the top of her voice. The guard glared and muttered into his walkie talkie. Shox stood firm under pressure. Peering into the Arrivals hall, he looked carefully at the men till he spotted a portly man with a handlebar moustache. As soon as the man appeared, Shox bowed low and belted out his rehearsed lines. 'Mughal-e-azam! Shehenshah! Badshah! Mumbai mein tashreef laaney ke liye shukriya. Ayiye! Padhaariye! Aapka sipaahi aapko uthaaney aaya hai!'

The camera swung to the office gang exploding with merriment. Shox looked so comical, Bala had doubled up in mirth. Then things took a serious turn. The guard summoned the police. Chaos followed. Two burly cops lifted Shox and dumped him unceremoniously on the pavement.

Mini went hysterical as the young visualizer told her how they had all raced to clamber into the closest cabs. She rewinded to the part where the policemen were carrying Shox away and fell back helplessly in her chair, shaking with laughter.

Her door opened and Shox walked in. The visualizer bent low and proclaimed. 'Mughal-e-azam! Shehenshah! Badshah! Mumbai mein tashreef laaney ke liye shukriya. Ayiye! Padhaariye! Aapka sipaahi aapko uthaaney aaya hai!'

There was a sudden silence. Behind Shox was Rustom, looking like a thundercloud. Mini sucked in her stomach to hide her paunch. It had become a reflex action, set off automatically each time Rustom was in a fifty metre radius around her. The rest of the office suddenly found urgent work to attend to. Even Shox slinked away.

A grim-faced Rustom turned to Mini. 'What's all this about? Why was my intern sent to the airport during work hours? And where did you send the office car, may I ask?'

Mini told him about the prank that had been played. But clearly, Rustom was not pleased.

'You are a very senior member of the staff, Mrs Mehta. Soul Mates expects you to be more responsible,' he stated, in clipped tones.

Mini bristled. 'It was all in fun, Rustom. You don't have to be such a stuffed shirt,' Mini said, trying to defend herself.

'This is an office, not some circus. When I am not in, I expect you to take over, maintain discipline and ensure that the juniors do their work,' Rustom went on.

Mini suppressed a strong urge to stick her tongue out at him. The man didn't have a sense of humour, she thought to herself. Deepa and she had played so many practical jokes on Mahatta in the Delhi office and he had never taken offence. And how dare this man talk to her like she was some subordinate of his?

Mini stood up. 'I thought you were a fun guy, one of those

rare men who could take a joke, but you are just a suit after all. A suit will always stick up for a suit, I should have known,' she said. 'And please, you are not my boss so don't behave like one. Let's see some respect around here. This place runs on creative steam. If I walk out of Soul Mates today, where will that leave you and your fancy PowerPoint presentations?'

Rustom looked explosive. 'I *am* the head of the office. And I will not condone my staff being sent on wild goose chases during office hours!' he bit out, through pursed lips.

Mini was past caring now. He was talking as though the entire episode was her personal idea. 'Yeah? And your secretary can do your son's homework in office, downloading pictures of Australian animals? That's very productive use of office time?' Mini shot back.

An ominous hush settled. Mini could hear the others in the office catch their collective breath. Rustom walked up to the door and shut it. Turning towards Mini, he gave her a baleful look. 'After everything I confided in you, about my wife being bedridden and all, I expected some sympathy from you, Mini. I actually thought we could be friends, maybe more. I can see that I was wrong,' Rustom said, and strode out of the room.

Mini felt tears pricking her eyelids. She had stamped out the romance even before she had lit the spark.

The office felt like a punishment posting for the next few days. Mini was so miserable, she even contemplated sending in her resignation to Mahatta. Rustom and she were not on speaking terms anymore. Work became impossible. The choreographer phoned, wanting to speak to her about the swayamvar music. Mini asked for the call to be directed to Rustom. The proofs for the invitations arrived, but Mini didn't have the heart to check them. The daft intern requested that she delete the airport footage from her laptop memory. Mini did it without a murmur. She was so upset, her appetite vanished. That was the only good thing to come out of the airport episode, Mini thought. Heartbreak worked brilliantly for weight loss.

Time dragged. Work suffered. So did Mini. Finally, she made up her mind. She would apologize. Not for aiding and abetting an office prank, but for being bitchy about the homework on Australian animals. She opened her email and started typing.

'Hi. Am sorry for mentioning the Australian animals. Shouldn't have got personal. Will download pix and make chart of African antelopes and deliver to school, if it helps. Truce?

M.'

A reply appeared a few moments later.

'Am sorry too, for being a stuffed shirt.

Dinner tonight? I know a place that serves outstanding pate fois gras.

R.'

Mini felt the clouds part and the sun appear. The cold war was over. Rustom had thawed. She did an impromptu jig and hugged herself. Her mobile trilled. She leapt to it, thinking it was Rustom, but it was only Shyam. The tiresome man had a knack of calling at the wrong time. Mini answered the phone reluctantly.

'What is it Shyam? I'm busy,' she spoke quickly.

'Nothing ... I was just wondering how you were getting along ... I should be in Mumbai next week. Is there anything you need from Delhi?' he enquired.

Shyam, in Mumbai? No way, Mini thought. He was the last person she wanted to meet in Mumbai. 'Oh no, I'm doing fine, I don't need anything at all. And why are coming? Who will look after Polka? She needs you more right now, Shyam. I can take care of myself,' she offered, wishing Shyam would put down the phone so that she could go and check herself out in the loo. She didn't want to look under-dressed for dinner with Rustom later on.

But Shyam was in no hurry. 'I'm missing you Mini. Can't you cut your trip short? I think the maid is having an affair with the guard. I don't know how to handle it, you better come back soon.'

Mini heard him out with grim satisfaction. Finally, Mr Mehta seemed to be realizing her worth. Let him suffer, she thought heartlessly, as she made some comforting noises and disconnected the call.

Mini had overheard Sandra making reservations for 7.00 p.m. so she knew that they would go for dinner straight after work. No time to change, Mini thought. But there was time for a quick blow-dry though. Mini sneaked out to the salon down the road, hoping to squeeze in a manicure as well.

They sat surrounded by intimate whispers, dimmed lights and liveried waiters. A man at the piano played dreamy melodies from Broadway musicals. Mini felt beautiful, her freshly washed and styled hair falling silkily around her face. Seated comfortably, she even forgot to tuck in her stomach, enjoying the mellow music and a single malt. Who would have thought, that one day, she, Mini – married, harried, working woman – could have a romantic almost-liaison with a Greek god? She peeped slyly at Rustom. He was looking right at her. Mini's heart skipped a beat.

'Are you all right?' he enquired, tilting his head. Mini nodded. 'So then, why so quiet and demure? What happened to the trickster who goes around trapping interns?' he asked smilingly.

Mini blushed. She didn't want a reminder of their earlier fight.

'Tell me Mini,' Rustom continued. 'How do you get all these

crazy, whacked-out ideas? What really goes on in that devious little mind of yours? What are you thinking about, right now? Hatching up another plan, this time with me as the victim?' he ribbed.

Mini pushed her hair back with one recently manicured hand. 'Oh no, I am not telling,' she replied with a smile.

'So how do you like working in Mumbai? I have a good mind to steal you and keep you here forever,' Rustom said, grinning.

'Why? Why should I come to Mumbai?' Mini asked, playing along. 'The Delhi office is much nicer, the people are so warm and friendly and I've got family there.'

'You don't think the Mumbai office is warm? Here you've got the head of the office dancing at your fingertips. What more do you want?' Rustom mocked.

Mini was enjoying flirting with this good-looking man. 'What about my husband? He won't let me come here. As it is he's miserable without me,' Mini parried.

'He'll cope, believe me. Husbands are a hardy breed. Look at me … my wife's been bedridden for weeks, but I'm managing just fine,' Rustom said with a shrug. 'And we'll find you a man here, what say?' he quizzed.

Mini's heart somersaulted. 'And where would we find such a man?' she enquired, trying her best to raise one eyebrow.

Rustom looked into her eyes. 'Well, I would gladly offer my services, but what to do, I'm a married man.'

Mini's heart sang. For the first time, she felt that she was getting somewhere. The man had feelings for her!

Abruptly, Rustom changed the topic. 'Tell me more about your husband … has he always been an entrepreneur?'

Mini told him about Shyam's family business of steel pipes and conduits. His father had run it with an iron hand, not allowing Shyam to alter the old-fashioned business procedures till recently, when he had suffered a stroke. Shyam had computerized some of the systems, though he had retained the dilapidated office in Khari Baoli.

'Hmm ... so he is a khandaani businessman. How did he get hooked up with Mad Mini?' Rustom mused.

Mini bristled. He had touched a raw nerve. From childhood, people had dubbed her 'Mad Mini'. As if being creative and insane was the same thing. 'Speak for yourself, I'm quite sane. It's you Parsis who are crazy, getting married to your sisters and brothers.' The words slipped out before she could stop them.

Neither of them spoke for a bit. Mini picked up her glass and took a huge gulp. Rustom leaned forward. 'Not all of us get married to people of our choice the way, perhaps, you and your husband did. Some of us have entirely unromantic encounters. Our marriage was arranged by our parents. Yes, she is my first cousin. We played together as children, went to school together, grew up together and then got married.'

He stopped talking as the waiter arrived with the soup. 'The bouillabaisse, Sir?' he asked deferentially. Rustom nodded. Placing a clear coriander soup in front of Mini, the waiter backed away silently.

Mini picked up the threads of the conversation. 'That sounds so sweet and reassuring,' she said. 'At least this way there are no rude surprises, you already know everything about the other person,' she opined, watching Rustom taste his soup. She loved to watch Rustom in a restaurant. He made a fascinating study, the way he twirled sips of wine, sniffed cigars and breathed in smoked cheese. A far cry from Shyam's crude, klutzy mannerisms.

Rustom looked at Mini. 'Well yes, there are no surprises, but there is no sense of discovery either,' he said thoughtfully. Mini grimaced.

'Well, Shyam and I met very romantically. We happened to be sitting in the same compartment in the Bangalore Express. It used to take two days and two nights to reach Delhi those days. We got talking, borrowed magazines, that sort of thing. I didn't suspect anything. Then, on the second day, Shyam proposed and threatened to jump off the train if I didn't accept. I had no choice. Refusing would have amounted to abetting murder. When we came back, he told his parents and in three weeks we were married.'

Rustom gazed at Mini. 'You are one lovable and special lady,' he said. Mini eagerly waited for him to say more, but the next course arrived. For a while, both of them were busy with the food. Rustom reached over for the salt cellar. Their hands brushed. Mini could have sworn she felt electricity.

It was getting late. The restaurant was emptying out slowly. But Mini wanted the evening to go on forever. Looking at Rustom, mischievously, she spoke. 'Well, you're not doing too badly on the lovable and special scale yourself. All the women in the office are crazy about you!'

Rustom grinned. 'All the ladies? Including you?'

Mini felt flustered. 'Except me,' she said, finally.

'Really? That won't do! What do I have to do to get you interested? Jump off a building?' he joked.

Mini pretended to be busy with the dessert menu and refused to reply. Little does Rustom know, she reflected, all he has to do is crook his little finger and I'll drop everything and go running to him.

By the time Rustom dropped Mini home, they were friends. A degree of camaraderie had been established. They could relax in each other's company. Rustom was so easy to be with, Mini thought. Even if things didn't work out as she wished, at least she had made a friend. Small consolation, she knew.

# 4

The airport incident had snowballed into a crisis. Someone had taken a photo of Shox in his airport costume, printed posters and put them up in the cafeteria. For some reason, Shox was convinced that this was Mini's idea. The sad part was, Rustom thought so too.

'Stop picking on the kid, Mini. Enough is enough,' he told her.

Mini tried hard to clear her name but no amount of explanations served to change his mind. The entire office knew that the young visualizer was the central character in the plot. Mini's role was only a supporting one. But there was no convincing Rustom. Angry and flustered, Mini developed a huge dislike for the intern. The feeling was mutual. Mini could sense animosity every time he was within three feet of her cabin.

Later in the day, Rustom walked into her room, frowning. 'Did you order bright yellow toilet paper with saffron streaks, for the hotel rooms?'

'Of course not,' Mini said. 'I clearly remember asking that the toilet paper be kept out of the colour scheme.'

Rustom asked Sandra to send in Shox with copies of the files sent to the printer. Shox shuffled in, put the files on the table and slipped out, looking like butter wouldn't melt in his mouth. Rustom went through the papers.

'There are no such instructions here, Mini,' he said, looking at her unblinkingly.

Mini thought quickly. She had not written down the instructions for the toilet paper but she did remember instructing the intern. She smiled charmingly at Rustom. 'Obviously, your intern omitted telling the printer about the toilet paper. But it's my fault, I should have put it on email or called the printer myself. Awfully sorry, Rustom, won't happen again.'

Rustom frowned. 'Well, someone will have to pay for this. This is expensive stuff. And completely useless. I'm afraid I'll have to debit it to your salary,' he said.

Mini was horrified but tried to look contrite. 'Come on! A no-budget wedding can absorb a bit of toilet paper,' she said.

'We do have an audit you know,' Rustom reminded her. 'Of course, you can keep the rolls,' he said with a shrug.

'What am I going to do with five hundred rolls of yellow TP?' Mini exclaimed.

'We can keep some in the office toilets, and the rest, I'm sure you'll find some use for it,' Rustom quickly said and left, shaking his head in bemusement.

Mini was incensed. This time, Shox had gone too far. If there was one thing Mini prided herself on, it was her professional competence. By intentionally making her look inefficient in Rustom's eyes, Shox had overstepped the limit. Moreover, this was insubordination. He had deliberately overlooked her instructions on the toilet paper. And to add insult to injury, she would actually be paying for his mistake. This time, Mini was not going to spare him. Shox had to be taught a lesson.

The Soul Mates office was small and well knit. Birthdays and anniversaries were celebrated with a little party and a token gift, bought with contributions from the staff. Mini remembered shelling out hundred rupees for Shox's birthday. Now, it was payback time.

In the evening, she asked the young visualizer to stay back for some urgent design work. Mini had noticed that the relationship between Shox and the girl had been steadily deteriorating. Shox was forever trying to boss over the girl. Mini had to get up every now and then and walk past their desks, the way the army does a flag march to keep rioters warned. She knew she would have a willing accomplice in the girl, for what she had in mind.

After the office had emptied out, Mini brought out the rolls of yellow toilet paper and summoned the visualizer into her cabin. Together, they fashioned saffron-yellow streamers and reels which Mini got the guard to hang from the ceiling. The potted plant at the entrance was given special attention; the young art director covered it in little yellow ribbons. Next, they cut out letters spelling 'HAPPY BIRTHDAY SHOX!' and stuck them on the front door. Twenty-five rolls went in wrapping the birthday boy's chair from head to toe. As a finishing touch, Mini took a cake knife from the pantry and tied a pretty toilet-paper bow to it.

The office actually looked brighter. Mini warmly shook hands with the visualizer and left for the day.

On her way into the office the next morning, she almost collided into two shady-looking men, carrying out a large gunny bag. Mini was just wondering if it could be a dead body, when a roll of yellow toilet paper fell out of one of the sacks. This needs investigation, she thought.

She walked in, went up straight up to Shox, pecked him soundly on both cheeks and wished him a happy birthday. If looks could kill, Mini would be that dead body in the sack. Heads peeped over several work-station partitions and Mini could hear smothered giggles.

Breezing past Sandra, Mini went up to Rustom. 'Good morning, what do we have lined up for the day? Any important meetings?' she asked, twirling the single red rose in the vase on his desk.

Rustom looked at her and sighed. 'Mini, will you get off that poor kid's case?'

Mini batted her eyelashes. 'What did I do? Don't you think the décor is really brightening up his day? Besides, think of the innovative use we have made of waste,' she said.

Rustom snorted. 'You are a real handful, Ma'am. I don't know what you'll be up to next,' he stated, shaking a finger at her.

'By the way, who were the two people carrying gunny sacks out of the office?' Mini asked.

Rustom smiled. 'They were from the Sulabh Shauchalaya. I decided to get rid of the rest of the toilet rolls before you found some other "innovative" use for them,' he replied, eyes twinkling. 'You are terrible for office discipline, Mini. One of these days I'm going to have to put you across my knee and give you a good spanking,' he said.

'Oooh, I can't wait,' said Mini, wiggling her ample bottom as she trundled back to her cabin.

Mini was thick in the middle of finalizing décor themes when her phone buzzed. It was her Delhi neighbour, Pritam Pal Singh.

'Hallo, Miniji, laang time, tussi te sannu bhul gaye? Vary bad ji. Aaj shaam da ki program hai? I insist, dinner saadey naal karo, changa?' Mini tried to turn down the invitation but Pritam wouldn't take no for an answer. She ended up giving him Aditi's address, promising to be ready at 8.00 p.m. It gave her a good excuse to leave early and miss out on Shox's birthday party. He may just stick the knife into her when he saw the ribbon on it, Mini thought.

She was getting into her salwaar-kameez when her phone rang. Mini ran a comb through her hair and rushed downstairs. Pritam Pal ushered her into his Honda City. She had barely got her seat belt fastened when he took off, driving so thoughtlessly, Mini spent the entire ride clinging to the door handle. By the time they reached his hotel, she was a jangling mass of nerves. She needed a drink, and how, Mini thought.

Pritam Pal's family was ensconced in the penthouse. It was good to see Sweetie's cheerful face again. When she hugged her affectionately, Mini felt like she was back home in Delhi. Sweetie put Mini through an exacting question-answer session. She wanted to know everything that was happening with Mini. How did she like Mumbai? Did she really have to work when it meant living so far away from home? Were the men in the office decent? Didn't she get anything to eat at Aditi's, why did she look so drawn and pale? Mini was thoroughly relieved when an attendant arrived with a tray, carrying a bottle of whisky and an ice bucket. She had joined a new gym lately and a drink or two would be easily balanced by some extra time on the treadmill.

Pritam Pal carefully removed a glass from the cabinet behind him, poured himself a generous drink and sat down, crossing his legs comfortably. 'And what will you have, ladies? Juice, nimbu paani or lassi?' he enquired, magnanimously. Mini gave up and asked for Pepsi.

It was the right choice, Mini told herself. The fizzy drink settled her stomach and she felt much better. She had been reluctant to accept the invitation, but meeting Sweetie and Pritam actually felt good. They talked about how terrible a city

Mumbai was and how much more beautiful and comfortable Delhi was. The conversation turned towards Mini's work and she told them about the wedding. Pritam became agitated when she mentioned the horses at the prince's stables. 'Oye he may be *prince* but I am *king*, Mini ji! King of Doberman!'

Mini was intrigued. How did someone become King of Doberman?

'I didn't think you were from a royal family, Pritam. You've never mentioned it before,' Mini said, fascinated.

Pritam laughed a belly-booming laugh. 'You, Paaabiji, always joke making! I am best breeder of Doberman dawgs in the India! I am Doberman King!' he explained, like a proud father.

Men and dogs, thought Mini. They shared the kind of kinship a man and woman could never quite manage.

She discovered that Pritam was part owner of a kennel in Chandigarh. He, along with his partner, imported rare dog breeds and entered them in shows all over the country. Sweetie beamed as Pritam waxed eloquent. 'Nobody in India can breed Doberman like I can ... they win every round in every dawg show,' he declared.

Sweetie laughingly told her that there were at least two dozen in their Delhi farmhouse at any given time.

'Two dozen puppies? That's a lot of work!' Mini exclaimed, horrified. 'Who looks after them, you or Pritam?'

Sweetie looked shocked. 'Me, of course! Aisey kaamon mein mardon ko kya pataa hai?' she asked, as she gave Pritam a shy, loving look.

Mini figured that in Sweetie's book, Pritam Pal could do no wrong.

Dinner was oily, heavy, spicy and heavenly. All thoughts of weight loss flew out of the window as Mini tucked in greedily.

Sweetie kept plying her with more, till Mini reached bursting point.

'Eat eat. Living so far away from your family, working so hard, you should look after yourself. Bimaar ho jaana hai nahin toh,' Sweetie fussed, giving Mini a pitying look.

Pritam nodded. 'I'll be going to Dilli next week to pick up my Dogo Argentino. I will tell Shyam – "Ye bhi koi baat hui? Paabhiji ko akela chhod diya, itney badey Bambai mein?"' he tsk-tsked.

Mini quickly changed the topic. 'Dogo Argentino? Is that a drink?' she asked. Pritam was scandalized. 'Oye tussi Dogo Argentino nai jaan dey? Canadian Dawg breed, paaabhiji! We will breed it in Chandigarh and sell da puppies. Very good-looking, strong dawg,' he explained as he showed her pictures on his mobile.

According to Pritam, the Dogo Argentino was the sardar of dogs. It had been originally bred to be a fierce game dog but it also turned into a cuddly pet once inside the hunter's home. Pritam obviously felt a keen sense of kinship. Mini formed a mental image of a dog with a turban and had to hide her smile.

When it was time for Mini to leave, Sweetie was almost in tears. In spite of herself, Mini too felt bereft. For the first time in Mumbai, she had experienced homely warmth and hospitality. Maybe she was missing home a lot more than she thought.

Pritam dropped her back, driving like a maniac. He screeched to a halt so suddenly outside Aditi's building, the food in Mini's stomach threatened to eject. Rushing up the stairs, she bolted to the bathroom and threw up.

Safe in bed, with a mug of hot water in her hand, Mini found her thoughts turning to Pritam and Sweetie. They were simple and old-fashioned but there was a genuineness about them that was utterly endearing. Mini thought about Sweetie cleaning dog poo with devotion. Someone like Sweetie would never think of any other man. How wonderful, reflected Mini, to be happy with what you have been given, never wanting more, never needing more. Sweetie's Prince Charming was Pritam; it was as simple as that. She loved him just the way he was. As for Pritam, if he ever looked at another female, it would be a Doberman. Something to think about, Mini figured, as she took two tablets of Paachak Pudina and switched off the lamp.

She woke up in the middle of the night as she felt something poking her back. It was the door handle from Pritam's car. She had somehow yanked it off and brought it home.

* * *

Next morning, even though she was feeling nauseous, Mini got dressed and left for work. It meant spending time with Rustom and time was running out. When she was with Rustom, Mini felt desirable, even sexy. He had that effect on women, Mini mused. After the dinner and conversation they had shared a few days earlier, she was hopeful that he liked her too. Could their mutual liking grow into something more? Mini crossed her fingers and sent up a silent prayer.

Late in the day, Rustom came to Mini's cabin. He wanted to discuss menus. Mini groaned. Her stomach had been making strange noises; she was paying dearly for her binge at Pritam's place the previous night.

They poured over the dozens of dishes offered by the seven-star resort where the wedding dinner was to take place. The prince had indicated that he was looking for originality – dishes that no one had savoured in Mumbai before. When Rustom asked her for suggestions, she could only think of ajwain-namak, heeng goli and imli churan. He shook her by the shoulder. 'Come on, what's happened to my girl? I thought she's never at a loss?' he said.

Mini was in a somnolent haze, wishing she hadn't gorged on Sweetie's paranthas. She tried, but could barely keep her eyes open. Rustom watched as her eyelids drooped. The lady could hardly hold her head straight. He asked Sandra to go home. He himself would wait till Sleeping Beauty woke up.

Rustom gently patted her cheek. Mini opened her eyes, nervous and panicked. Rustom wanted to give her a hug. She straightened up. 'Why did you let me doze off?' she demanded to know. Mini was petrified that she had been dozing with her mouth open or worse still, snoring.

Rustom grinned. 'You looked so sweet, like you were waiting for your Prince Charming to come and kiss you awake. I didn't want to disturb you,' he said mischievously.

Mini turned her face to hide her expression. Why didn't you kiss me awake, Rustom, don't you know, you could be my Prince Charming, she thought, her heart beating madly.

She got up and went to the bathroom. Sitting on the toilet seat, she got the perfect idea for the wedding dinner. It always happened. The throne was very conducive to brainwaves. When she returned, Rustom was winding up for the day. But Mini was in no hurry to go home.

'I have an idea for the dinner menu,' she said.

Rustom sat down, all attention. 'Instead of figuring out exotic dishes from all over the world, how about we go for jungle cuisine?' she proposed.

'Go on,' Rustom nodded.

'See, our theme is swayamvar, right? So it's about all these warriors in the forest, making their way to the swayamvar. And later, after Prithviraj carries away Samyukta, they hide in the jungles, trying to ambush him. So that's why we should have jungle cuisine,' she explained, with a flourish.

'Yeah, but what about the menu?' Rustom asked, looking confused.

She should have guessed, Mini thought. Production people couldn't recognize an idea unless it was spelt out for them, item by item, making for easy budgeting.

She sat down. 'Okay Mr MBA-in-a-suit, how about this? We do jungle cuisine ... in other words ... game. The kind you kill on shoots. Rare pheasants from Austria, ostrich from South Africa, venison from Botswana, partridges from the Kutch ... get the picture, Dodo?'

Rustom was impressed, Mini could tell. She continued. 'We'll fly down traditional cooks from Rajasthan, Zulu chefs from Cape Town, Kiwi chefs from New Zealand ... "no-budget wedding", right?' Mini finished.

'How do you do it, Mini? Are you sure you don't think up ideas at home at night and pretend to get brainwaves?' he asked, incredulously.

'Practice, darling, practice. I've been doing weddings for so many years, brilliance has become routine,' she replied nonchalantly.

'Well, all I can say is that you should stick with it, you are good at what you do. Tell me – and don't you breathe a word to anybody about this – if I were to go solo and start my own wedding-planning outfit, will you join me?' Rustom asked.

'Make me an offer I can't refuse and I shall think about it,' said Mini teasingly.

'How about a drink to seal the deal,' Rustom invited. 'I could do with a drink, but no deal yet,' Mini said, even though it seemed like the perfect idea, she thought. Rustom could get the business and she could run it. It would be almost like a marriage.

'Where to?' she asked, as she slid into the passenger seat of Rustom's car.

'It's a surprise,' Rustom eased the powerful sedan on to the road. He pressed a button on the music system. Soft music filled the car. It was just the other day, Mini reflected, that Rustom had picked her up from the airport. They had become so comfortable with each other in such a short time. Is that what having a soulmate felt like, Mini wondered, smiling at Rustom.

He stopped the car. They were in front of an old building. Mini followed Rustom as he locked the car and entered the lift. By now Mini had figured out that they were going to Rustom's home. She almost backed out. The last thing she wanted was to sit and survey Rustom playing doting husband to wheelchair-bound wife. But it was too late. The lift doors were opening to the second floor.

Rustom let them in with a key. Mini followed him in, feeling out of place. He ushered her to a sofa and disappeared. Mini was on edge. The wife could wheel herself into the room any moment. Would she be able to tell how besotted Mini was with her husband?

Rustom's home was lovely. A piano sat sedately near the window that opened out into a large balcony. Polished wooden furniture was arranged in an understated, elegant manner. Family portraits adorned ornate frames. An antique grandfather clock chimed. Mini looked up to see Rustom walking towards her, carrying a tray with glasses. He had changed out of his office formals and was dressed in track pants and a casual tee. She was just going to ask about the wheelchair when Rustom spoke.

'My wife and son have gone to her parents' house for a while. She felt she would recuperate faster there. There's nobody to look after her here,' he explained.

Mini was secretly delighted. If the wife was out, and a man brought you to his home, surely it meant something, she thought, her heart racing expectantly.

'I thought we would be more comfortable here than in a pub,' Rustom said.

Mini sat back, leaning into the sofa. Today, she knew, would not be a repeat of her experience in Pritam Pal's penthouse. Rustom would mix her drinks exactly as she liked them.

She asked for a mojito and Rustom whisked the ingredients in a silver metal shaker, complete with crushed ice. An intimate silence followed till Rustom cleared his throat and started the conversation.

'Mini, how do you like living in Mumbai now? Getting used to it?' he asked.

Mini made a face. 'I don't think I'll get used to it, frankly,' she said. 'It's very smelly, very dirty and very expensive.'

Rustom grinned.

'Don't laugh. My salary disappears so quickly, I have a good mind to start moonlighting,' she finished.

'Don't you go doing that, Mini,' Rustom said, sounding scandalized. 'I can't have my creative head moonlighting under my nose! Anyway, you are too good for that sort of thing,' he said.

Mini was pleased by his response. Rustom obviously held her in high regard. 'If you really want to make some money, I have a plan,' Rustom offered. 'Do you have any idea how much money Mahatta makes out of us? Guess how much profit he will make from the royal wedding alone?' he asked.

Mini shook her head. She didn't have a clue. 'Come on, take a guess,' he prodded.

Mini felt a familiar panic rise in her. Numbers always did that to her. She had problems with simple addition, leave alone guessing Mahatta's turnover. She hazarded a wild guess. 'Er ... a lakh?' she asked.

Rustom looked at her disbelievingly. 'At least fifty lakhs!' he revealed. 'That's more than your salary and mine combined. Doesn't that make you mad?'

Mini nodded, vaguely, not quite sure why she should be angry with Mr Mahatta.

Rustom elaborated. 'Mini, you've got so much experience and I have plenty of contacts. I've even sounded out my uncle and he is willing to finance me till I find my feet. Why don't we think about starting our own venture instead of giving it all away to Mahatta?' Rustom said, looking at her, eagerly waiting for her response.

So he is serious about setting up his own company, she thought to herself. She sighed. What was all this talk about new companies, when all she was looking for was a new relationship?

'I'll take care of all the details, find you a spacious flat through my Parsi network,' Rustom continued, taking her silence for concurrence. 'You'll have to move to Mumbai, of course.'

'No way. Shyam is not going to agree ... he's a Delhi boy and his entire business is set up there,' Mini said, quickly. She didn't want Rustom to get his hopes up for nothing. 'Besides, his cricketing buddies, his family, they are all in Delhi! Why would he move?'

The doorbell rang. Rustom answered it and came back with a stack of cartons. Mini could see an expensive restaurant's name on them. This man was so considerate, Mini thought, as Rustom emptied the food into delicate chinaware and brought it to the centre table on a tray. Mini made a half-hearted attempt to get up and help, but Rustom shushed her and pushed her back on the sofa.

'I know how tired you are. You were so sleepy, I thought I'd have to carry you here. Now sit back and let me pamper you. We can't have the creative head all washed out and neglected! Else god knows what you will go and tell Mr Mahatta back in Delhi. As it is, the man is completely nuts about you. "Mahatta darling, that Rustom is such a slave driver, sack him na..."' he said, mimicking her voice with a twinkle in his eyes.

Prodding her slippers off her feet, he gently lifted them up and put them on the sofa. After serving her a portion from all the dishes, he propped the plate on her knees and stood looming over her. 'Now say grace like a good girl!'

Mini looked at the plate and salivated. They were all her favourite dishes. Juicy chicken chunks in dreamy, creamy spaghetti, drowned in melty, squelchy cheese. Freshly baked bread, pan-fried in generous dollops of finger-licky, garlicky butter. Broccoli and beans tossed with mustard, garnished with copious chunks of succulent pineapple. And she knew there was dessert to follow. Mini's entire being quivered in helpless anticipation.

She could get used to this, Mini decided as she tucked in greedily, loving every bit of the attention Rustom was lavishing on her. He had even made sure that she got the biggest chunks of pineapple, knowing how much she loved them.

All Shyam ever ordered was aloo. He actually wanted her to come back to Delhi because he was nursing a cold. The gall of the man, Mini thought angrily. But Rustom was by her side again, adding pepper to her pasta. 'Eat up ... you've been looking thinner since your first day in Mumbai. I don't want Mahatta accusing me of starving you. Though I must say, it suits you, this trimmer look.' High praise from the Greek god himself! Mini felt like the cat who'd licked the cream.

Replete with food, Mini slipped into a light slumber, her mind wandering. Rustom was adorable. But would she ever be able to live in Mumbai, long-term? He must like her at least a little, Mini thought, or else he wouldn't have been so attentive and caring.

Rustom shook her shoulder. 'Dreaming about me?' he asked, aping a corny underwear ad from yesteryears.

Mini blushed guiltily. 'No way, I was thinking about the choreography for the dance,' she countered.

'How very disappointing,' Rustom replied. 'You still haven't told me how you think of such utterly romantic ideas. Is it because your husband is very romantic ... or is it just your wild imagination?'

'Shyam? He's the least romantic person I know,' Mini replied.

'So it's a case of opposites attract, hmm?' he probed.

Mini pondered over the observation. Was she even attracted to Shyam anymore? Theirs was not a case of opposites attract, it was more like contrariness repels or something. 'Well, we've been married so long, I don't know any more,' she said, thoughtfully..

Rustom nodded. 'I've been married only seven years,' he said, as he neatly twirled spaghetti round his fork. 'Tell me, did you go through the seven-year itch? Is it for real?' he asked Mini.

She looked at him, a mischievous glint in her eye. 'Ah, so now I know, why you're sending the wife away, bringing me home and plying me with food and drinks! Seven-year itch!'

Rustom suddenly turned serious. 'Mini, you know, I really like you. I think you are hugely talented. If I wanted to indulge my seven-year itch, there are so many women around who would jump if I clicked my fingers. But you? You are special. I have too much respect for you,' he finished.

Mini didn't know whether to slap him or shake him by the hand. She should have been flattered but she was more like, shattered.

* * *

There was so much to be done and the deadline was looming large. Mini finalized menus, supervised choreography, checked artworks, approved designs, sampled dishes ... the tasks were endless. She sent out teams to get swatches of material for backdrops and samples of paper for menus. When they came back, Mini poured over them and then got Rustom to do budgeting exercises. Thereafter, since this was to be a "no-budget" wedding, Mini happily settled for the most expensive items. She was in her element, enjoying every bit of her day. The best part was, if she worked late, Rustom would stay back too, dropping her to Aditi's place later. Reason to be encouraged, but no point getting her hopes up just yet, Mini cautioned herself.

The swayamwar was foremost on her mind. After considering endless options, she needed to take decisions. It was time to do market visits, starting with the city's wedding malls. Rustom accompanied her to Mumbai's biggest wedding souk. Mini took pictures of the different kinds of garlands available, the garland being an integral prop in a swayamvar. She also made the most of the shopping opportunity, buying shoes and sandals by the dozen. Rustom was more amused than irritated.

'What are you going to do with so many?' he asked.

Mini gave him a wise look. 'It's a female thing. You'll never understand,' she said.

'All right then, Mrs Imelda Marcos, can we go check out the wedding gifts section now?' Rustom asked, shaking his head in bewilderment.

Who on earth was Mrs Marcos, Mini wondered. She sounded like one of those Santa Cruz women in short terylene skirts and nylon tights with ladders. They invariably wore matching pumps with their skirts. Did Rustom think of her like that? Her mood slumped. She excused herself and went to the rest room. Sitting on the WC, she went online on her phone and searched for 'Mrs Marcos' on Google. What she read made her smile again. After brushing her hair and applying a fresh coat of lip gloss, she walked out feeling like a queen.

She found him in the jewellery store, examining earrings. Was he going to buy her a gift? She went and stood next to him. The earrings he was looking at were traditional Polki danglers, with beautiful green-and-red stones embedded in gold. They were Mini's favourite kind of jewellery. She picked up a pair and held it against her ears, turning to the mirror.

Rustom's reflection joined hers in the mirror. He looked at her for a long minute. 'Hi, you look familiar. Have we met before? Mini! These earrings look beautiful on you!' he exclaimed. Mini's heart turned over at the look in his eyes. It had been so long since she had seen desire in a man's eyes for her. It was a heady feeling. She could get used to it.

\* \* \*

Shyam called up the detective agency's seedy office in Nehru Place, a worried frown on his face. Ever since his neighbour

Pritam had called up, telling him he had met Mini in his hotel bar, dressed in a nightie and smoking, he had smelt a rat. She was up to some tricks. What was she up to? And did she think that he would let her get away with it? No way. He was going to find out what it was and then bring her back home where she belonged.

The house hadn't been the same since Mini had left and Shyam was getting thoroughly tired of telling the maid what to cook and how many litres of milk to buy. Moreover, Polka's diet needed extra attention and, while he had started giving her almonds and tofu, he was sure that more needed to be done. The vet wanted Polka to go for regular walks but Polka was sluggish and unwilling. Mini would have known what to do, Shyam thought. But lately, Mini had been behaving really cold and stand-offish. Something was up, and he was going to get to the bottom of it, Shyam told himself.

* * *

The bridal chamber decor had been rejected, again. Mini was in a panic. This had never happened before. She had spent days researching, doing her best to replicate the period look. The team had slaved tirelessly. Now what? The client had been so happy at the idea of staging a swayamvar, Mini had not been prepared for any opposition.

She barged into Rustom's cabin. 'What's with this client?' she asked, angrily. 'Tell him to hire some other wedding planner! I can't handle this.'

Rustom looked up from his computer screen, the picture of calm. 'Relax Mini, the client is not rejecting your designs ... he is merely asking you to duplicate his,' Rustom said, as if talking to a petulant two-year-old.

'What do you mean he wants me to copy his? No way!' Mini was furious. These clients, all they had was money with no taste whatsoever. Her designs were original and brilliant, but they would rather have a cheap imitation. What rot!

'When you are feeling less angry, I'll tell you what the client proposed,' Rustom said, a maddening grin on his face.

'Angry? Me? Huh, catch me getting emotional over a design. Huh!' Mini sniffed. 'What has the client proposed?' she asked, after a pause.

'Sit down, Sweetheart,' Rustom said, pointing to the chair in front of his desk.

Mini sat down in a huff. 'Don't you sweetheart-darling me! It doesn't work,' she puffed.

'The prince wants the bridal chamber to be designed like the gazebo in his palace in Srirajmahalpur. He has invited both of us to be his guests at the palace, so that we can study the decor and design it accordingly.'

Mini was speechless. A whole day and a night away from the office, in a romantic palace, with Rustom! It sounded like the answer to her prayers. However, pretending to be unmoved, Mini sighed. 'Bloody clients, they think we have nothing better to do. The visualizer can go,' she said.

'Oh no, you need to go, Mini, the client has especially asked for you. I'll send that intern along, the one you like so much,' Rustom offered.

Mini saw a flash of red. So it was critical for the senior-most creative person to go, but Production could get away by sending the junior-most member of their team. 'If it's not important

enough for you to go, then how come it's so important that I go?'
she asked. 'Either the occasion demands senior representation or
it doesn't. You decide,' Mini said, as she walked out of Rustom's
cabin in a temper.

Back at her desk, she was still upset. What was wrong with
the man? Didn't he want to be with her? He seemed to find her
attractive enough. Then why wasn't he jumping at the chance
of them spending time together? And who did Rustom think he
was anyway, her boss? If she did go, she would be busy checking
out the palace for design input. Who was supposed to keep the
client occupied meanwhile? Rustom would have to come along
and do his job, Mini decided. Or else … or else Mahatta could
go with her! That was a thought worth pursuing, Mini figured.

She picked up the phone. 'Rustom, it's all right if you are
too busy to come to Srirajmahalpur. I'll get Mr Mahatta to join
me,' she said.

She could hear Rustom plotting murder. Five minutes later,
he was in her cabin. 'We take the morning flight on Saturday
and return on Sunday afternoon,' he said tersely. Mini bit her
cheek to hide her smile.

Saturday was less than forty-eight hours away. Mini was
in a tizzy. She had no time to shop. What would she carry as
nightclothes? Plus she needed a new pair of glasses. Though she
wore contact lenses all the time now, she had to remove them
before going to bed. Her bedtime reading was done in an old,
nerdy pair of spectacles. But this time, Rustom would be with
her; she simply could not be seen in her dowdy, schoolmarmish
frames. She'd rather go blind. Surely there were twenty-four-
seven lenses? She called her contact lens specialist in Delhi. No
luck. Only invalids and geriatrics were given permanent lenses.
They were unhygienic and dangerous, unless you stayed strictly

indoors or in a sterile environment. Mini thought about faking an illness, but there was no way she could avoid the outdoors. In any case, it was highly unlikely that Rustom would come visiting her in her room.

All the same, you never know, she thought, and decided to pack her naughty negligeé.

That night, Mini dreamt that she was riding a huge, black stallion, with Rustom sitting behind her. She leaned into his broad chest as he smoothed the hair from her brow. As he bent his head to kiss her lips, something cracked. Mini woke up, and realized, to her utter consternation, that she had worn her glasses to bed and cracked them beyond repair. She would have to manage with lenses alone now. It was all for the best, Mini decided. She would remove her lenses last thing at night and wear them first thing in the morning. Rustom would not see her in spectacles even by oversight.

★ ★ ★

Rustom had already checked in when Mini reached the airport. Mini saw him sipping coffee at the snack counter and her heart did its usual mad dance. The man was just so handsome, it was unfair.

He took her strolley from her and they walked to the security check. A bomb scare had occurred the day before and the place was swarming with uniforms. Mini went to the women's queue, almost skipping with joy as she thought of spending so much captive time with Rustom.

When she came out of the frisking booth to pick up her bag, she found that it had been kept aside. A lady policeman gestured to her to open it. Mini reluctantly fished the key out of her purse. The police lady threw aside the clothes in Mini's bag and triumphantly held up a gleaming, white, oversized bra.

'Ismey kya hai, maital detector kyun beep kar raha hai, check karney ka,' she stated. Mini went red, crimson and pale in quick succession. From the corner of her eye, she could see Rustom and other passengers peering at her. Her bra was holding up the entire queue. She could have died. Whoever invented underwired bras hadn't bargained for metal detectors. Mini told the lady to keep the bra and snapped the bag shut, glaring at the possé of male policemen who couldn't stop grinning.

Without waiting for Rustom, Mini marched away, dragging her bag behind her. She disappeared into the toilet, thinking glumly that she would be one bra short on the trip. She'd have to wash one and wear the other, she figured.

Mini was just fine till the plane took off. Rustom was seated next to her and she could get whiffs of his cologne. But as soon they were airborne, the familiar panic set in. As always, her mind threw up a succession of worst-case scenarios – the captain was not putting off the seat belt sign because something was terribly wrong ... all the stewardesses had vanished ... the plane was going to crash. She stole a glance at Rustom. He was calmly reading the newspaper. The plane lurched. Mini clutched the armrests of her seat, scrunched her eyes shut and waited for the crash.

She was saying her prayers and sending telepathic messages to Aditi and the gang when a warm hand placed itself on hers, squeezing reassuringly. Rustom was holding her hand. Mini thought she had gone to heaven. Could she have found her 'happily-ever-after' in the afterlife? The fear receded, to be replaced by a feeling of security and well-being.

How different Rustom was from Sicko Shyam. Every time

she took a flight with him, he pretended to be petrified himself, telling her that her weight would surely bring the plane down.

Reality intruded. A stewardess announced that the captain had switched off the 'Seatbelts On' sign.

Rustom's hand remained on hers. She looked at him, blushing. Rustom gave her a tender look. 'Fear of flying?' he asked. Mini nodded. 'Who would have thought? Big, brave Mini afraid of little clouds in the sky?' Rustom teased, giving her hand another squeeze.

Mini's heart soared. She was actually enjoying flying. It was a miracle. 'It's an irrational thing, I know. But I can't seem to help it,' she said.

Rustom turned to her and took both her hands in his. 'It's all right to be afraid sometimes, Mini. Everybody has some phobia or another,' he said, looking straight into her eyes.

Mini felt like crying. Rustom's concern had completely undermined her. Never before had a man shown so much consideration and respect for Mini's feelings. She was moved to the core. Romantic heroes did exist. Rustom was drop-dead gorgeous, successful, great to work with, awesome company and so considerate.

Mini stared out of the window, her eyes bright with tears. She was in love. And it was as beautiful as all the romantic novels had predicted. Yes, she wasn't even sure of his feelings yet. But she, Mini Mehta, esteemed wedding planner, had snatched true love from the jaws of menopause.

She would move to Mumbai, bag and baggage. Rustom and she would float their own company. But would she able to live in Mumbai long term? She thought about Delhi with its leafy avenues and sleepy by-lanes, the slower pace of life compared to Mumbai's manic bustle. After the sultry, unremitting stickiness of Mumbai, Mini actually missed Delhi's dry summer heat. No way, she decided. She was never going to leave Delhi. She would brave the aeroplane rides and come to meet Rustom on assignments and maybe, assignations. They could work together and that would give her more time to see where their relationship was headed.

The hostess started to come down the aisle with food and Rustom let go of her hands. She could still feel their warmth though, and she stored it away in her mind. It was a feeling she was going to relive again and again.

They arrived in Srirajmahalpur and were whisked away in an elongated car of vintage make. After an hour of driving through congested Srirajmahalpur, it reached a quieter, greener stretch. The car swept into a driveway lined with majestic ashoka trees. They were met by an ancient royal retainer in traditional garb. As they walked through an unending corridor that led to the guest rooms, Mini felt she had never been happier. With random people bowing to them and wishing them in hushed, reverential tones, she and Rustom became a couple. The palace staff seemed to think they were married.

The room Mini was to sleep in, seemed as large as a cricket pitch. She could hear her footsteps echo. Rather spooky actually, she thought. She peeped out to see Rustom's bag being placed in a room across the corridor. Well, one could always creep across if there were some ghosts at large, she told herself. Rustom would respect her fears.

Sipping a cup of tea in the balcony of her room, Mini found herself doing some wishful thinking. If only Rustom would reciprocate her feelings. If only he would steal into her room at night, hold her in his arms. They would spend the night making passionate love. Unlikely, she knew, sighing deeply.

But there was nothing to stop her, she figured. She could make the first move and seduce her man. The argument built up rapidly in Mini's head. Everything was fair in love, she reasoned. There would never be another chance like this. There was no better time or place. Life had thrown her an opportunity and whether she seized it or threw it away was up to her. Soon she would be back in Delhi with Sicko Shyam. Back to her humdrum life. And who would ever know? It would be her treasured secret ... some stolen hours with the love of her life. The wedding deadline was her personal deadline too. Because once the wedding was over, she would have no reason to stay in Mumbai. She would probably never meet Rustom again. Mini never missed a deadline.

Immediately, her mind began to visualize scenarios, as if on autopilot. It threw up ideas, evaluated them, incubated them, till the perfect one came along. When that happened, it was almost as if a *ping* sound happened in her head and she knew she had hit the jackpot.

Her first plan was to act perfectly normal and disinterested all along. Then at night, when everyone had retired, she could go to Rustom's room, pretending she had a headache. As he rummaged in his bag for a Disprin, she would fall onto the floor in a faint. The rest was up to him.

Too obvious, Mini dismissed the idea. She would have to think of something more subtle. She went inside to pour herself another cup of tea. A disapproving ancestor stared at her from a painting on the wall, his droopy moustache and heavy-lidded eyes giving him a menacing appearance. Mini hoped he wouldn't start sleepwalking at night.

Sleepwalking? Now that was an idea, Mini thought. She could sleepwalk to Rustom's room!

Yes, that was it, Mini decided. She was just figuring out the exact modus operandi when her phone rang. It was Shyam, cropping up like a bad penny as usual. She picked up, yawning loudly, hoping he would take the hint.

* * *

Shyam was on edge. Mini's phone had been out of reach all morning. Aditi had informed him that Mini was on a flight. Mini on a flight? She hated flights. Who was she with? Where was she going? Frantic, he had been trying her number every few minutes. Finally, he had got through.

'Mini, where are you? Who are you with? Why didn't you tell me you are going out of town?' Shyam bombarded Mini with questions. But there was no response other than a solemn silence. Shyam forced himself to calm down. 'How was the flight? Are you okay?' he asked.

'Never been better!' Mini replied.

Shyam was taken aback. Mini was never in a cheerful mood after a flight. What had happened to change that?

'Why, what was so special about the flight?' Shyam queried.

'Well, a colleague of mine was on the same flight, we are travelling for design-related work and there was so much to discuss…' Mini trilled.

Shyam's worst suspicions were confirmed. Mini was seeing someone. 'Really? I think it's time we discussed a few things too. I'll call you when you are back in Mumbai,' he said and disconnected in a rage, leaving Mini holding the phone with the engaged tone beeping rudely in her ear.

Shyam's boorish behaviour did nothing to dampen her spirits. She washed up, changed, applied fresh war paint and went downstairs to meet Rustom.

The palace manager was waiting to show them around. A golf cart stood at the porch. Mini waited for the manager to sit down first. She still remembered how a similar contraption had tipped over once, when she had tried to sit in the back seat.

The golf cart trundled down a picturesque path. A peacock croaked in the bushes. After fifteen minutes of being jolted and jerked about, they stopped outside a smaller building. The manager led the way inside, explaining that this was the king's pleasure palace. Mini blushed as Rustom gave her a broad grin.

A gazebo stood in a corner of the garden. The manager pointed towards it. 'These are the frescoes that His Highness wants you to see. Please take your time looking at them. The driver will take you back when you have finished,' he murmured and stood back politely.

Mini walked into the gazebo, curious to see what was so special about it. After all, all her designs had been rejected in favour of this one. Rustom was already taking pictures of the exterior.

Nice but not thrilling, Mini decided. The walls were intricately painted, depicting scenes from court life. The colours were rich and abundant, but even so, the whole effect was rather underwhelming, Mini thought.

Rustom walked in, zoomed his camera lens on the paintings and snickered. As Mini looked at him, he started to chuckle. What was the joke, Mini wondered. Was she wearing her shirt inside-out?

'What's so funny?' she asked, sniffing. 'Don't tell me this tame, traditional pavilion is the reason all my designs got thrown away?'

Rustom gave her an amused look. 'You don't see it, do you?

Tame indeed! Open your eyes and look, Mini! You're missing something!'

Baffled, Mini walked closer to the wall. 'What's so interesting about a man getting his feet washed while a woman … *oh my!*' She was dumbfounded. They were erotic paintings! How could she have missed it? The entire pavilion was painted with men, women and yes, horses, birds, all entwined! And what was that huge thing that woman was holding? Could it be … yes it was … an elephant's dick!

Mini was embarrassed and amused, in equal measure. Amusement won. She snorted. Rustom responded with an answering guffaw. A huge laugh began to rumble in Mini's belly and escaped. She laughed and laughed. Rustom joined in, pointing at the figure of a woman bending, with a horse standing on his forelegs behind her. Mini keeled over. This was hilarious, she thought, wiping tears from her eyes. These decadent princes! She loved them, she did, Mini decided. Her mind raced. She would modernize the existing design, make it more in sync with the general wedding colour scheme and add some scenes from the swayamvar theme. How graphic or subtle should she make it? Mini wondered what the prince would prefer. How on earth would she find out?

Rustom was busy taking close up shots of a man in an impossible back-twist with a woman sitting astride his shoulders. He had a huge smile planted on his face. Mini looked at him and love surged inside her. Amazing, how unabashed and natural she was with this man, she thought. It was a good thing that Shox hadn't come along, he would have been embarrassed beyond words. She could guess how Mahatta would have reacted.

'Chhee chhee, ye kya ho raha hai? Miniji, aap aankhen bandh keejiye please.' As for Shyam, he would have grossed her out completely, with some crass, tasteless comments. With Rustom on the other hand, she could have a good laugh over just about anything, even dicks.

Back in her cricket-pitch room, Mini changed into her nightclothes and removed her contact lenses. She climbed into bed but sleep eluded her. Her mind was wide awake. It was painting pictures of Rustom in bed, his hair tousled and face relaxed, handsome and irresistible in repose. And here she was, just a few feet away, doing nothing about anything. She had to seize the moment. She got up before she could get cold feet. Soon now, she told herself. She would sleepwalk her way into Rustom's bed. He would take her in his arms, kiss her and they would proceed to put the gazebo gymnasts to shame. Removing her pyjamas and tee, Mini slipped on her naughty red negligeé and felt her way to the bathroom. Squinting at the items in her toilet kit, she sprayed on a cloud of perfume. She was ready.

Mini tiptoed into the corridor. Everything was still and silent. She was feeling her way along the wall to find Rustom's door when she heard the rustle of clothes. She looked up. Peering down the corridor myopically, she saw the outline of a man, arms stretched out, walking towards her. Mini's heart tripped. Rustom too hadn't been able to resist her! He was coming down the corridor to her room. This was the moment she has been waiting for her entire life. Mini wished she had her contact lenses on, so she could clearly save the image for posterity. Rustom was coming closer. Mini ran her hand through her hair, pinched her cheeks to give them colour and assumed a provocative pose. He was just a few feet away. Mini closed her eyes and held up her lips to him in a sexy moue.

She waited. Nothing happened. She waited some more. Finally, she opened her eyes. Rustom had vanished. She turned around and saw a blurred view of his back as he continued walking down the corridor and disappeared round the corner.

Mini was heartbroken. If this was Rustom's idea of a joke, Mini thought, he was a cruel man. He was making fun of her. He didn't care or else why would he make a mockery of her feelings? Tears rolled down her eyes. She hated Rustom. Making her way back to her room, Mini crept into bed, her thoughts awhirl. She had made a big, fat, fool of herself. How could she even think that a man like Rustom would be interested in her? From now on, her relationship with Rustom was going to be strictly professional. No jokes, no repartee, no camaraderie and certainly no love.

The tears wouldn't stop. It was as though a dam had burst and long-suppressed feelings were spilling over. Was she ever going to make it with her Dream Lover? She had come so near, and yet was so far. It was all Shyam's fault, she decided. If he had been even twenty per cent like Rustom, she would have been able to make do. But he was so gross, so unromantic, so cricket-mad and dog-crazy. How could she fulfill her romantic fantasies with a man like that? On the other hand, what Rustom had just done to her was inexcusable. She wondered if he cared for her at all or if she was just a huge amusement factor in his life. Either way, the joke had gone too far, Mini decided. She was going to snap all ties. When the wedding was over, she would cut herself loose. Wiping tears, Mini fumbled for the jug of water on the bedside table when she remembered she had forgotten to apply her anti-wrinkle face cream. She almost got up, then decided that neither Rustom nor Shyam were worth the effort. Instead, she reached into her bag and brought out her Linus's blanket – an extra-large bar of nougat-filled chocolate. It never failed to work. With every bite, its creamy texture soothed away the pain and anger, leaving Mini in a sweet cocoon where the world couldn't get to her.

She woke up sometime later, feeling uncomfortable. There was a hand on her left shoulder. Mini sat bolt upright in terror. She was going to reach out for the light switch when the hand gripped hers. Mini froze, then melted. She couldn't believe the sudden reversal in fortune ... Rustom had come to her! As usual, she had condemned him, prima facie, without waiting for proof. The moment she had been waiting for all her life, had arrived. Mini willed herself to relax, her nerves tingling with joy. Rustom was trying to kiss her neck and it tickled. His moustache needed trimming, Mini thought, smiling.

Moustache? Rustom didn't have a moustache! Mini leapt out of bed in a flash. This wasn't Rustom. Who could it be, Mini thought frantically, as she pushed the person away. Desperately wishing she could see properly, Mini was just about to scream when the person got up and walked away. Just like that. With his arms stretched out ahead of him.

It was most insulting. It had taken barely any persuasion to kick the man out. Her eyes burning with tears and strain, Mini went back to sleep, feeling sorry for herself. Twice in a night was a lot of rejection to take.

In the morning, Mini was at the breakfast table before Rustom. She tipped half the bowl of sugar into her cereal and was moodily pouring milk into it when he arrived. His loud and bright 'Good morning!' had her on edge immediately. How could he be in such a good mood after he had given her such a bad night, Mini fumed. She decided she wasn't going to say a word. Let him talk to the walls, she told herself, because she was not going to listen. She had her lenses on now and could clearly see the dastardly man for what he was.

Rustom tried several times to make conversation but Mini was too hurt to respond. They drove to the airport in complete silence. On the return flight, she made sure she had a seat as far away from his as possible. How could a man be so considerate when she confided her fear of flying to him and so indifferent when she gave her heart to him, Mini thought bitterly. They made it back to Mumbai, Mini sitting with her eyes clenched throughout. Mercifully, it was a short flight and ended without crashing. Mini hailed a cab and left for Aditi's place, without bothering to wait for or say goodbye to Rustom.

As the driver sped away, Mini thought about how the Mumbai sojourn had toughened her up. She could now take cabs alone, walk into places by herself and handle bank work without help from Shyam. All she had to do was toughen up on the inside and she would survive heartbreak too. She had made huge strides in self-confidence, surely that counted for something, she figured, her mood lifting somewhat.

She decided to put her newfound self-assurance to work. Leaning forward, she asked the cabbie to stop at the nearest liquor shop. Fifteen minutes later, she had a pint of chilled beer in her hand and was drinking to the end of her so-called romance with Rustom.

Aditi wasn't at home when Mini arrived. She toyed with the idea of going out for dinner, when she remembered that the best cure for heartbreak was ice cream. She ordered butter chicken, butter naan and daal makhani from a nearby takeaway along with a giant tub of Death by Chocolate.

By the time she had showered, eaten and settled down in front of the television, eating scoop after scoop of chocolate ice cream, Mini's angst had melted into melancholy. The soppy rom-com distracted her for a bit. It had Julia Roberts walking out on her lying, cheating boyfriend. Mini felt much better knowing that even pretty women like Julia faced man trouble.

Mini shut herself in her cabin the next day, refusing to talk to anyone at all. Her only communication with Rustom had been a terse email first thing in the morning, asking him for the photographs of the pavilion so that she could initiate work on the design. When she checked after an hour, his mail was waiting for her, accompanied by a heavy attachment, containing the pictures. She checked to see if he had written a contrite apology – not that she cared – but there was none. At the end of the attachment was a movie clip. Mini clicked to open the attachment. Her heart stopped as she stared at the screen in disbelief.

It was a scene inside the palace in Srirajmahalpur. A man was walking down the corridor in front of her room, with his eyes closed, arms held in front of him. He seemed to be sleepwalking. But it wasn't Rustom. It was the palace manager! Rustom had captured him on camera. Then a horrid thought occurred to her. Was she on camera too? She scanned the clip with her heart in her mouth. Luckily, Rustom had recorded the sleepwalker before she had arrived on the scene. She and her red negligeé were nowhere in sight. Mini heaved a sigh of relief.

Her senses leapt with joy. It was not Rustom she had seen on that fateful night; it was the sleepwalking manager of the Srirajmahalpur estate! He must be the one who had come to her room that night – the mystery man with the moustache. What a comedy of errors the palace incident had been. And she had been blaming Rustom for being heartless. She really would have to get a new pair of glasses. They had almost cost her the love of her life, she thought, as her heart flooded with tenderness for Rustom. He hadn't turned his back on her. Rather, she had turned against him, for no fault of his.

Quickly, she dashed off an email to Rustom. 'Sorry for being crabby and moody. Blame it on biological rhythms. The sleepwalking manager is too much! How did you manage to get him on camera? What on earth were you doing prowling around the corridor in the middle of the night? Or did you have an amorous assignation that you haven't told me about? Fess up. M.'

She pressed the send button and waited for him to reply.

Her laptop pinged almost instantly. 'I couldn't sleep so I was taking night shots of the palace for future reference. Your bio rhythms are difficult to fathom. What can I say? Hope the bridal chamber design is coming along fine. Regards, Rustom.'

Rustom was piqued, Mini could guess from the tone of his email. But then, he had cause to be. She had been unreasonable and grossly unfair. From now onwards, she was going to rely on her feelings, not on what she saw. Her eyes, rather her broken spectacles, had led her to believe the worst about Rustom. Now she would see only with her heart.

\* \* \*

As the wedding date grew close, the pace of work in Soul Mates picked up. Days flew past in a flurry of reconnaissance trips.

Mini asked Rustom to take her to the private beach where the swayamvar was to take place. She wanted to set up the swayamvar on the sand, under the moonlit sky. Rustom accompanied her to the venue. The beach was gorgeous, Mini thought. Miles of clean sand, blue skies and tastefully planted palms. But it wasn't the kind of beach that she associated with her childhood memories. Cotton candy, popcorn, camel rides, sand castles – these made beaches what they were. She shared her thoughts with Rustom and he was thoroughly amused.

On the way back to the office, he turned towards Juhu Chowpatty, just to give Mini a taste of what she was missing. When Mini saw the quasi-mela that was a perennial part of the beach, her face lit up with excitement and she clapped her hands like a child. Rustom laughed at her and went off to buy cotton candy and popcorn.

When he came back, she was kneeling on the sand, building a castle. He smiled. Mini looked up. 'Come, I could use some help,' she invited, looking like a chubby little schoolgirl in a candy store.

'What are you building?' he asked her.

'I am making a replica of the bridal chamber,' she replied, her eyes full of mischief, holding up two nicely rounded pebbles. He joined in the game, creating sand figures in obscene postures. Mini, pretending to be shocked, found candy wrappers to cover them up. Gosh, he hadn't laughed so much in a long time, Rustom thought, as they shared cotton candy and ice cream.

Mini spotted a tiny island a short distance away from the beach. Rustom gallantly offered to take her there but Mini knew he was joking. She sat down on the sand with eyes closed, enjoying the cool sea breeze. May as well take a quick nap, she figured. The early-morning gym class meant that she was often sleepy by afternoon. She dozed off, only to be woken up by someone yelling out her name. Mini got up in a hurry and quickly checked her hair and lipstick in her cell phone screen. And then she spotted Rustom.

Oh my god, she thought, look at him! He was astride a water scooter, trousers rolled up to the knees, no shoes. He was stunning and so sexy. Mini's heart began to beat wildly. He yelled out her name again and Mini walked towards him, trying to look unmoved. Revving the water scooter, he patted the back seat, shouting for Mini to sit pillion. There was a rakish grin on his face and his eyes shone with excitement.

Mini slipped out of her high heels and strapped herself into the life jacket he was holding out. She was standing hesitantly at the edge of the water when a strong gust of breeze sent her skirt flying up, like in the classic Marilyn Monroe moment. She frenetically peeled it off her face. Good thing she was wearing brand new panties. She yanked the skirt down and looked at Rustom. He was staring unabashedly. Mini felt herself go beetroot red. 'I can't! My clothes will get wet!' she yelled, holding on to the skirt.

Rustom leered at her playfully. 'Then take them off! Come on, I'm taking you to the island!'

Mini stepped gingerly into the water, scrambled on to the back seat of the scooter and sat astride. Her skirt climbed up from both sides, revealing creamy, plump thighs. Rustom stared at them. Mini tried to pull the skirt down but didn't quite succeed. The scooter took off with a jerk, throwing Mini against Rustom's back. She clung to his shoulders, hanging on for dear life. Rustom was enjoying himself. He was racing the scooter, twisting it from side to side, making Mini cling to him all the more. He threw his head back, leaning against Mini's breasts. Mini tried to move away but shot back up as she almost slid off the scooter. Mini hadn't experienced this kind of heady excitement in a long, long time. Throwing caution to the winds, she moved closer to Rustom, placing one hand on his left thigh. Rustom's head snapped back up. He straightened, pointing to a cluster of rocks in the distance. 'There's your island, Ma'am! Have a good look before I turn back for the shore!'

He switched off the engine as Mini gazed at the rocks. 'I wish I could go to that island and stay there forever! Just me, the waves, the breeze … no worries, no commitments,' she murmured.

Rustom smiled. 'Great idea. I'll come along, to keep you company. You cook and clean, I'll collect firewood and catch fish.'

Mini's heart stopped. Rustom was obviously joking, but the look in his eyes was serious. This is crazy, Mini thought. The man was married, he was aware that she was married. Why would he talk about moving to an island with her? Plus she didn't really want to move to an uninhabited island; she hated cooking and cleaning. On the other hand, moving anywhere with Rustom, even to hell, was a dream come true.

Rustom turned back to the shore. Neither of them spoke a word till they reached the spot where Rustom had parked the car. Mini was deep in thought. She did want to have a relationship, but she didn't believe in sex for the sake of sex. She wanted a beautiful episode – something to cherish and hug to herself on nights when Shyam snored too loudly or when he picked chicken out of his teeth with fingernails. Something that made her believe that Mills & Boon romances did happen, even to women like her. It was not about sex, it was about romance. It was about finding a soulmate, versus being stuck with a marriage partner.

It was not as though Shyam was a bad husband. Far from it. He was a good provider. They lived comfortably. He made a loving father to Polka, spoiling her, bending backwards to fulfill her every whim. Mini cared for Shyam and was dependant on him in many ways. It was just that their marriage had degenerated into some kind of listless, mechanical routine, where they went to office, came back, ate, slept, then left for work again the next morning. The excitement had fizzled out, never to return. She knew that Shyam cared for her and she was certain that there were no other women in his life. But let's face it, Mini mused, neither one of them was exactly thrilled to see the other any more. Shyam just didn't make her heart beat faster. On the other hand, Rustom did. All he had to do was look at her and she was a quivering mass of nerves. But he was married too. Mini wondered what he really felt for her. Was he actually willing to move to an island with her? Leave his wife, his job, and his parents? Or was she just a colleague to him, a useful person to know in the industry?

It was all rather confusing. Mini took her problems with her to bed that night, telling Aditi she had a headache.

\* \* \*

Shyam was in the detective agency's office. Detective Mahesh was giving him details of Mini's constant companion in Mumbai. A man called Rustom, who worked with her. He stared at a photo of the man. Mini's taste had really gone to the dogs, he thought. A callow youth, no chin, no moustache ... what was Mini thinking?

Detective Mahesh was reeling out fact after fact. 'Comes from rich Parsi family, Sir. Only son. Married to his cousin. One child. Educated in a Parsi school. Studied hotel management in Lausanne, Switzerland. Had worked in the hotel line for nine years before joining Soul Mates as production head.'

Shyam butted in. 'Yaar, tell me something hidden, something his wife wouldn't know. Like, has he had any affairs?'

Detective Mahesh continued his litany. 'Non-smoker. Likes fine whisky, western classical music and women. Relationship with wife is not very good. Confirmed flirt. Known for sleeping with women in his work place...' Shyam did a double take. Detective Mahesh continued, '...especially attracted to women in fishnet stockings and short skirts...'

Shyam stood up and stopped him with an emphatic bang on the table. 'No danger here, then. Mini never wears skirts!'

'You better take a look at these, Sir.' Detective Mahesh said, quietly pushing an envelope towards Shyam.

Shyam saw the first picture and sat down. It was Mini, dressed in a skirt and stockings, the skirt riding up her thighs, laughing as she clung to the back of a man, on what looked like a water scooter. There were other pictures as well. Mini in track pants, emerging from a gym. Another one of her in a flattering full-length dress, being helped into a car by that blackguard, Rustom.

'Put me on the next flight to Mumbai,' he barked into the phone to his secretary, pocketing Mini's pictures as he strode out of the detective agency.

★ ★ ★

An exultant Mini stood on the scales in the personal dietician's clinic. She had done it! A long spell of staying away from ice cream and chocolate was being rewarded. The needle had moved. She was several kilos lighter! That called for a celebration. Aditi suggested a shopathon and Mini agreed at once. A new wardrobe was the need of the moment. This time, Mini thought, she was not going to let the weight come back. Her current wardrobe had clothes in four sizes. Almost-fat, fat, very fat and humongous. Mostly, she oscillated between very fat and humongous. Now, a new category had been created – almost-sexy. Soon, she would graduate to the size that had eluded her since her college days – DDS – drop-dead-sexy.

Mini decided to go the whole hog and throw in a visit to a hairstylist. She would get a new cut, something younger and hipper. Aditi recommended a salon in Bandra. Mini walked in at the appointed time, trying to look like the decisive career girl that she was. The hairstyling diva, who ran the place, looked up desultorily from the head she was working on and asked, 'When did you last wash your hair?'

'Just before coming here,' Mini replied. Surely a hair stylist could tell freshly-washed hair from dirty?

The stylist called out to one of her minions. 'Wash, with two conditioner rinses!'

Sitting in the salon, wrapped in a plastic sheet, hair wet and falling in rag tails, Mini felt the morning's elation seep out of her. It was almost like the sexy hormones had been washed away, along with the non-existent dirt in her hair. Unless those hormones had been non-existent too, she thought unhappily.

Finally, the diva came up to her. Standing behind Mini, surrounded by a troop of adoring assistants, she appraised Mini's face. 'Something to make the jaw look slimmer ... hide the double chin ... bangs, maybe?' she muttered. The assistants nodded vigorously.

'Not too short,' Mini ventured weakly. Nobody paid attention. The diva had forgotten the head beneath the hair. Mini closed her eyes. When rape is inevitable, lie back and enjoy it, someone had once said. She was undergoing 'The Rape of The Lock'.

Half an hour later, Mini opened her eyes. Who was that in the mirror? Was that her? So chic and young! Rustom would love it, she just knew!

The diva gave her an amused look and deigned to speak to her. 'Use a good conditioner, regularly. And come back in three months.'

Mini walked out of the salon on cloud nine. Aditi ooh-ed and aah-ed for a good ten minutes when she saw her. It felt really good to be admired, Mini thought. Worth all the dieting and gymming she had gone through. Especially so if it made Rustom stop in his tracks.

As luck would have it, Mini didn't get to meet Rustom all week. He was away at the client's office, finalizing budgets. But Mini needed to spend time with him as they had an important presentation coming up. She asked Rustom to drop by at her flat on the weekend so they could knock off some urgent stuff. Besides, she hadn't had a chance to show him her new haircut. Mini knew that Aditi would be in Lonavla on Sunday, on her monthly visit to her mother's old-age home. She asked Rustom to come by eleven. They could work for a couple of hours and he could go home for lunch if he liked. Rustom agreed, offering to bring Chinese takeaway that they could eat together.

Sunday dawned and Mini was full of anticipation. She could hardly wait for Aditi to leave. As soon as she did, Mini rushed out to buy flowers and arranged bunches of them all over the apartment. Putting her favourite Begum Akhtar CD into the player, she locked herself into the bathroom for an indulgent, languorous bath. She swiped a razor over her legs, arms and underarms, tweezed her eyebrows, bleached her upper lip and smoothed lotion onto every inch of her body. Slipping into a slim, black skirt and a tailored blouse, she emerged in a cloud of scent and vapour. She teased her newly cut hair into shape and brushed it till it shone, applied light make-up and perfumed all the hollows of her body. She was ready. It was a quarter-to-eleven. Rustom would arrive any moment. Mini re-arranged the red roses in the vase on the side table, breathing in their heavy fragrance. She placed a small pot of lemongrass oil in the incense burner and kept a bottle of Rosé in the wine cooler. Picking up the jars of cornflakes, pickle and chutney from Aditi's tiny dining table, she put out a cheese platter and a slab of smoked Gouda, knowing how partial Rustom was to it. As a finishing touch, she sprayed a floral room-freshener around the room, just in case the Wankhedes down the hall decided to fry fish. She was putting mouth-freshener on her tongue when the doorbell rang. Mini did a quick check in the mirror, sprayed on a little more perfume and opened the door, leaning against it seductively.

She looked up breathlessly. And couldn't believe her eyes.

Standing before her was Sicko Shyam, a greasy paper bag stuffed with batata wadas in one hand.

Mini froze. 'What are you doing here?' she lashed out.

'Can I come in at least?' Shyam said indignantly, pushing past her into the room. 'You look horrible! What's all that red-red colour in your hair?' he asked accusingly.

Mini bristled. 'I've had a trim. And those are streaks.'

Settling down on the sofa, Shyam looked her up and down. 'Lost some weight, have you? It doesn't suit you. Neither does this new hairdo weirdo. You look like that annoying character from the Comedy Central show.'

Mini could have cheerfully killed him. Throwing down the bag of batata wadas on the table, Shyam picked up a piece of smoked Gouda and began chewing it. Mini was desperately trying to send a text message to Rustom, asking him not to come. Shyam spat out the cheese, a piece landing in the red roses that Mini had arranged so lovingly.

'What's this stuff … some diet thing? Disgusting! Come, I'll take you out for some real food. Let's get some lunch.'

Mini was too busy texting. She didn't reply. Shyam got up and tried to snatch the cell phone from her. 'Who are you messaging, let me see. You see your husband after so long and this is the way you react?'

Mini dashed into the bathroom and slammed the door on him. 'Wash your face while you're in there. Who are you all made up for anyway? Expecting somebody? A boyfriend maybe?'

A furious, frustrated Mini yelled out through the closed door. 'Nobody! I just adore being the butt of your jokes. By the way, why are you here? Did you come all the way from Delhi just to comment on my new look?' Mini turned on the tap, ran the flush, and in the resultant din, frantically called up Rustom.

'Rustom, Mini here. We won't be meeting today, something's come up. I'll see you tomorrow at work. Bye.' Mini disconnected without giving Rustom a chance to speak.

Standing with his ear to the door, Shyam heard every word and made up his mind. She was talking to the blackguard. He would have to take swift action. When Mini emerged from the bathroom, he declared loudly and firmly. 'Yes, I've come all the way from Delhi, to take you home. We are booked on the evening flight. Call your boss and start packing.'

Mini was aghast. 'I'm *not* going back. The great, big, royal wedding is right around the corner! No way can I leave now!'

Shyam was taken aback at her vehemence. He tried a different tack. 'The maid quit.'

Mini looked up. 'Then I'm definitely not going back.'

Shyam started to plead. 'I have to buy the vegetables myself and count out clothes for the dhobi. I'm suffering, Mini!'

'Serves you right!' Mini said, starting to enjoy herself. 'The bedsheets haven't been changed since you left,' Shyam whined.

'Why didn't you change them? Do they remind you of me?' Mini asked, somewhat mollified.

'I don't know where you keep the clean ones!' Shyam blurted out and Mini hardened her heart again.

'Oh! You're disgusting! And selfish! So insensitive! Shyam, at least sometimes get a wee bit romantic. We are meeting after weeks and the only reason you're missing me is because the maid has quit? Please leave. I can't deal with you. You horrify me! And bang the front door shut behind you when you leave.' Mini locked herself up in her room.

Shyam sat down once again, miserably chewing on a batata wada. He had made a hash of it, he knew. He should have met her head-on with the pictures he had got from the detective. But he knew his wife only too well. Confronting Mini was like waving a red flag at a bull. She would never forgive him and would probably have an affair just to get even with him. Plus, he was sure that the whole thing was not Mini's doing. She was too innocent, his Mini. It was that Parsi who was leading her astray. And no wonder, because Mini was looking so good. He had been stunned. Was this his Mini? So sexy, slim and svelte? But the transformation had not been for him. She had done it for some Parsi bloke. That was what had made him lose his cool, when he had seen her at the door, posing like that, looking so hot. What did she see in that Parsi, Shyam wondered. Hadn't he been a good husband to her? Where had he gone wrong? Did she feel nothing for him any more? Okay, so he wasn't romantic, but Mini knew that, didn't she? She had accepted him the way he was. Or had she? Well, if romance was what it would take to win her back, he would be romantic, Shyam decided. He would woo his Mini. But what about the Parsi? Maybe it was time to have a word with Mahatta. Mini would have to come back to Delhi, no two ways about it, Shyam determined.

Mini spent the next day in the beauty salon, getting the auburn streaks in her hair dyed black. Shyam's comments had really hurt, more than she cared to admit. His unannounced appearance the previous morning had shaken her to the core. What if he had arrived after Rustom had come? She couldn't bear to think about it. Crazy as she was about Rustom, she didn't want to hurt Shyam. He was harmless and simple ... not a mean bone in his body. So, what now? Mini mulled over the situation as she waited for the colour to take effect. It wasn't her fault if the man of her dreams had appeared in her office. She hadn't gone looking. Rustom had just happened to her! But was she ready to leave Shyam? What about Polka and her pups? And the house that she had bought with Shyam? The questions in her head were driving her crazy. She gave up. If something was meant to happen, it would. She would cross her bridges when she came to them. And she would deal with Shyam when she could spare the time. Right now, there were a gazillion things to be done before the royal wedding got off the ground.

The design team would be taking over the swayamvar venue the following week and Mini needed to get a fix on some things before handing it over to them. Rustom and she were scheduled to visit it in the afternoon.

Her imagination went into overdrive the minute the car entered the resort gates. 'The chariot will come in from there, and all along here, here, here and here, there will be models throwing petals on the bridegroom,' she told Rustom, as they slowly made their way from the driveway to the front porch.

'Okay, you got it,' Rustom murmured, hurriedly taking notes.

Mini stepped out of the car and walked briskly to the other end of the porch, Rustom in tow.

'I want a water wall along this side,' she said, trailing her fingers on the surface of the wall.

Rustom looked up from his notes. 'A water wall?' he said, a twinkle in his eyes as both Mini and he intoned an imitation of Mahatta. 'What an idea, Mrinaliniji! What an idea!' They laughed, happy with the spontaneous way they had both come up with the mimicry.

'That man is a real character,' Rustom said, grinning.

'I know. One of these days, I'm going to write a book on him – *Mahatta: The Soul of Soul Mates*,' replied Mini, making Rustom smile again.

She walked ahead, staring into space. 'Do you think ... elephants ... no, camels ... no... too common ... I know! Dogs!'

'Where?' Rustom asked, a hint of nervousness in his voice. He was terrified of dogs.

'Black dobermans ... we could hire them from Pritam ... or *hey*! Black Siamese cats! On golden designer leashes!' she exclaimed, very excited.

'Where? What?' Rustom asked, rather alarmed.

Mini was getting carried away. 'Four behind the chariot, four in front!'

Rustom sighed. These creative types were all stark raving mad. Schooling his expressions, he wrote down in his notebook. 'Eight Siamese cats. Done,' he murmured.

Mini was feeling great. Her mind was as sparkling as ever, no dulling or blunting there, Mini told herself with a self-satisfied smile. Feeling generous, she turned to Rustom. 'If anybody can arrange all this, you can! You're the best production head I've ever worked with,' she said.

Rustom was suitably flattered. 'Thank you, Ma'am!' he replied, gloating. 'I keep telling you, let's start our own shop, we make a crack team!'

Mini sailed through the front doors and into the hotel,

Rustom trailing a few steps behind. She paused in the lobby. 'Rustom, go back, walk in from that door again,' she ordered.

Rustom obediently went out and entered again. Mini stood, deep in thought. After the swayamvar on the beach, the traditional varmaala would take place inside. Mini was trying to see out how the event would unfold. As Rustom walked towards her, she began walking towards him, taking tiny steps, very bride-like.

'Come on, you are my groom! Look excited!' Mini teased, as she walked.

Rustom's eyes glinted. 'My beautiful bride! I can't wait to ravish you!' he said in a mock whisper, joining in the game.

Suddenly shy and confused, Mini withdrew to safe territory. 'Good. We need to tell the choreographer how much area she has to work with,' she said.

But Rustom hadn't finished teasing her. 'Tonight, you'll be mine. At last!' he leered. Mini felt herself go hot and cold all over. When she was right in front of him, Rustom took his office access tag from his neck and slipped it over Mini's head like a garland, his hands on her shoulders. They looked into each other's eyes, lost.

'Sir, would you like to see the private dining area now?' A hotel executive enquired, clearing his throat.

Mini and Rustom followed the executive into the hall, both silent and withdrawn.

That night in bed, Mini wondered how it would have ended if the executive hadn't arrived and broken the spell.

# 5

Mini stood in front of the bathroom mirror, examining herself critically. All that stood between her and a great body was five kilos, give or take a few. If the lights were off, the stretch marks would be invisible. The overhanging stomach was a bigger problem. Corsets were not quite the answer. They could disguise but could not deceive permanently. Maybe it was time to invest in a tummy tuck? Or lasers? Or Botox? Or all of them?

The physical difficulties could be dealt with but the social ones were trickier. There were whispers all around. She could sense eyes following her. Mini was certain that she had overheard Sandra calling her a shameless hussy. Was it was so obvious, her attraction to Rustom and their growing closeness? But why should she care, Mini thought defiantly. She was away from her hometown, in a city where not many people knew her. If anyone had to worry about reputation, it should be Rustom. She was simply looking for her last hurrah before menopause. When it was over, she would go back to her life in Delhi, Mini decided, as she sucked in her cheeks and tried to highlight her cheekbones.

\* \* \*

It was late in the evening. The office was almost empty. The design for the bridal chamber was ready. Mini had kept the graphics bold yet sophisticated. Rustom had walked by several times, waving the to-do list. They needed to sit down and take stock. Mini was deep in thought, trying to figure out if she could get horses with blush-pink manes for the bridesmaids, when Rustom walked into her cabin. She didn't hear him coming and he stood for a moment, staring at her. She looked so cute. Hair unkempt, top button come loose, eyes dreamy, all curled up in her chair. Gosh, she was sexy. He wondered how she would react if he heaved her up from the chair and kissed her deep on her blush-pink mouth. She had the hots for him, no two ways about that. Maybe it was time he did something about it?

Mini looked up, saw Rustom and blushed. Rustom smiled. 'Tired? Want to discuss our to-do list over coffee?' Mini stretched. Another button popped open.

Rustom swallowed. 'Let's go to the coffee shop down the street. We can discuss deadlines and then I'll drop you home.'

Mini picked up her bag and followed Rustom out, rejoicing at the prospect of spending time alone with him.

Rustom ordered two cappuccinos. Mini asked for sweetener. They went over the list, item by item. Mini gazed longingly at the strawberry pastry calling her from the confectionery counter. It looked like it had just the right amount of gooeyness and cream. Her mouth watered. Resolve weakened. Just one little pastry couldn't do much harm, could it? Rustom asked if she had frozen on the colour and graphics for the trousseau packaging. 'Blush pink with sugar on the top,' she blurted, her mind still on the pastry. But Rustom was staring at her lips. Mini's heartbeat quickened. The diet was working. She quickly aborted the thought of the strawberry pastry.

It was getting late. Mini looked up from the laptop screen, stretched and suppressed a yawn.

'Sleepy?' Rustom enquired.

'Yeah. I hate marriages,' Mini said with a grimace. 'Come on, you are a happily married woman,' Rustom said, giving her a quizzical look.

'Happily married? That's a myth,' Mini said lightly.

Rustom nodded. 'Yeah, who needs marriage, except for wedding planners? All it does is tie you up in knots,' he said.

The coffee had left Mini wired up. 'It's up to you to free yourself,' she challenged.

'But I can't do that,' Rustom said softly.

'Can't or won't?' shot Mini.

Rustom was silent.

Forever torn between the two ... the story of our lives, Mini reflected, staring moodily into her cup. 'Should we always do what we should? What about what we want?' She spoke aloud.

'So ... what is it that you want?' Rustom asked, giving Mini a piercing look.

Mini recalled a forgotten piece of poetry. She quoted,

'"The meadow and the mountain with desire

Gazed on each other, till a fierce unrest

Surged 'neath the meadow's seemingly calm breast,

And all the mountain's fissures ran with fire."'

Rustom was all attention. Putting his hand on Mini's, he pressed home. 'I know just the place.'

'So what are we waiting for?' Mini asked breathlessly.

Rustom lost his nerve. This was going too fast. Mahatta would sack him for this, he thought. 'I need to pay,' he deflected, looking for his wallet.

'I don't charge,' Mini shot back.

Rustom beckoned the waiter, who arrived with the bill. They walked out of the cafe, the tension between them so tangible, you could slice through it with a cake knife.

Getting into the car, they drove in silence. Mini's heart was bungee-jumping. Was Rustom actually taking up the invitation she had so clearly offered? Was she going to let him? Well, that was a foregone conclusion. She had been waiting for this moment all her life. And she was prepared – freshly manicured and liberally perfumed. She cast a sidelong glance at Rustom. He was concentrating on the road. Mini closed her eyes and willed herself to breathe normally.

When she opened her eyes, she found herself outside a small, inconspicuous building, in a nondescript back alley. Rustom led her inside. Mini surreptitiously sniffed her underarms to make sure her deodorant was still working. Rustom pulled her close and planted his lips squarely on hers. All thoughts fled from Mini's mind as she froze on the spot.

They were at the company guest house, Mini realized, as she glimpsed the Soul Mates logo on the door. It was a musty, old, slightly shabby flat. Her heart beating nineteen to the dozen, Mini stepped into the bedroom. Rustom pushed her down on the bed. He was panting, fumbling with the buttons on her blouse. Quickly, Mini arched her neck to lose her double chin.

'Please switch off the light, Rustom,' she asked, petrified that he would see her stretch marks.

'Shy, Mini?' Rustom whispered.

Mini nodded demurely. He fumbled with the light switch and the room plunged into darkness.

Later, Mini thought that it was the darkness that brought out the demon in her. Because as soon as the light went off, she lost it. Deprivation made Mini greedy. She devoured him. Rustom was a box of chocolates and she was the kid in the candy store. He was the dessert buffet and Mini was the crazed glutton. He was lamb steak and she was a starving vagabond. She kissed Rustom with the full force of her hunger. He yelped. She shifted her lips to his ear, nibbling furiously. Rustom cried out in pain. The man did protest too much, Mini thought, sinking her teeth into his shoulder.

'Easy, Mini, easy. I'm not going anywhere. Slow down. Let me show you,' Rustom whispered as he nuzzled her ear, sending the most delicious sensations up her spine. His lips moved to her neck, then sucked gently on her lower lip. It was sheer torture.

Rustom was cupping her breasts, holding them like two plump muffins. Her nipples perked up, firm, like cherries on top. With his mouth on the cherries, he plundered Mini's body with his hands. She moaned in delight as he sucked greedily. She felt his hands moving delicately on her skin, like a feather-light mousse gliding deliciously over the tongue. Now squeezing, now dipping, playing havoc with Mini's senses, he had her longing for more. Mini had forgotten how good this felt, how much she had been craving the touch of a man.

When he reached out and put his hand between her legs, fingers moving, dipping, exploring, tasting, Mini surrendered the last vestige of subliminal guilt. And just when she thought she had died and gone to heaven, he moved his mouth and planted it on her lower lips. Mini curled her fingers in his hair and wished he would never stop. She closed her eyes and savoured the feeling, mindless with pleasure.

When Mini lost count of the number of times she had come, he moved up and thrust himself roughly into her. Mini felt as if she had fallen into a tub of melted chocolate, full of soft marshmallows and oodles of sinful cream.

Later, Mini lay back, feeling replete and absolutely full. All her life, she had been trying to fill an unknown void. Now Rustom had plugged the hole.

★ ★ ★

The guilt and horror came rushing in after Rustom dropped her off at Aditi's. She let herself into the empty flat, sat in the balcony and released a flood of tears. The contentment that had filled her, leaked out slowly. She should have been on seventh heaven. She had just slept with Dream Lover. She had fulfilled her mission.

Looking at it from another point of view, she had lain back and enjoyed sex like a shameless whore. Like someone famished. But was it really wrong to enjoy herself, Mini thought. It had been so long since someone had worshipped her body. Shyam didn't want her any more. It was ages since he had even looked at her with lust. What was a girl supposed to do, she asked herself defiantly. Rustom, on the other hand, had made delicious love to her. He had pleasured her like no one had, before. Was it so sinful, to fulfill her physical needs?

But what about true love, the need for a soulmate? She had wanted true love, not sex for the sake of sex.

It was all Rustom's fault, Mini thought. His behaviour had been appalling. After a day full of climax after climax, the end had come as an anticlimax. She had been waiting for a declaration of love. But Rustom had simply climbed off, pecked her on the cheek and hustled her out. No confession, no promises. Not once had Rustom said 'I love you' to her. She ought to have confirmed his feelings for her before sleeping with him. But she hadn't. What did that make her? Some sort of desperado? Was she using him? And was Rustom using her too, passing time while his wife was in a wheelchair? Besides, if she was really in love with Rustom, she should divorce Shyam.

Guilt and confusion crowded her mind. She had always believed that she had wanted romance, not sex. But here she was, having an illicit liaison in a sleazy guest house, on a bed that Mahatta probably slept in on his Mumbai visits.

This was not what she had been waiting for. She was a self-respecting, educated woman of refined tastes. No way was she going to settle for anything less than the real thing, a soulmate.

Mini made a firm decision. This was the first and the last time she would sleep with Rustom. Unless, of course, he loved her back.

* * *

After dropping Mini to her flat, Rustom went to his lawyer's place. The draft agreement for the partnership was ready. Now that they had slept together, convincing her would be a cinch. Together, Mini and he would set up north India's biggest and brightest wedding planning outfit.

He had so much in common with Mini, thought Rustom. Even their sex drives matched. If Nilufer wasn't in line to inherit her father's property, he would have moved in with Mini.

But at work the next day, Rustom kept to his cabin and Mini kept to hers. The royal family was coming to the office and both of them were kept thoroughly busy with their presentations. When Mini entered the conference room, Rustom was already there with Sandra, going through his slides. Both of them pretended that the previous night had never happened.

'So today's the big day,' Mini remarked.

Rustom nodded.

'Are you tense?' Mini asked.

'A little,' Rustom replied. 'This is our make-or-break account. If we can pull off this one, there will be no looking back, you know that.' Rustom said, as he straightened his tie.

Sandra left the room to answer her ringing telephone. Mini looked at Rustom, willing herself to ignore the sexual tension in the air. He leaned closer and whispered in her ear. 'Last night was sensational for me. And for you?' he asked. 'I can't wait to do it again, Mini. I want to push you down on this table and...' he said, breathing heavily and closing in on her.

Mini moved away, alarmed. The table was made of particle board; it would never take her weight. 'Why don't we discuss this later?' she said hurriedly, as Sandra came back into the room.

'Meet me in the bar at the end of the road after the presentation,' Rustom whispered in her ear. Mini hastily moved to the other end of the room, as far away from Rustom as possible, holding on to every semblance of willpower, even though all she wanted to do was forget about the presentation and take her chances with the table.

Rushing to the loo, Mini washed her face, combed her hair and gave herself a good talking to. She was not going to sleep with Rustom. Not now, not ever. She was crazy about the man. But sex for the sake of sex was not her style, she reminded herself. She was not desperate and she wasn't going to behave in a way that made her feel like a Slutty Sandra clone.

* * *

The presentation went off well and the client went away pleased. Everybody cheered. They all wanted a party. But now the real work would begin. Advances would have to be paid, costumes would have to be fitted, dress rehearsals would need to begin, a few Bollywood types would have to be bought. There were menus to be sealed, props to be hired, alcohol to be sourced. In the euphoria over the meeting's success, Mini felt panic mixed with excitement rising up in her, tying her stomach in knots. There was so much to do, how would they ever manage to pull off such a huge event in such a short time? She looked at Rustom. He was surrounded by jubilant Soul Mates employees. She glanced at her watch. It was time to go to the bar where Rustom had asked to meet her. But it looked as though Rustom would take a while. She sent him a text message, telling him that she would meet him in half an hour. They could catch the happy hour. As long as it didn't extend into After Hours in guest houses.

Mini made a quick detour to the beauty salon. Lately, her looks had become important to her. Rustom noticed everything. When she wore new earrings, he whistled appreciatively. When she bought new stilettos, he stared admiringly at her legs. And when she wore a new skirt, he confessed that it gave him inappropriate thoughts.

She reached the pub to see that Rustom was already at their favourite table, with a pitcher of draught beer in front of him. She sat down across him. He poured beer into their glasses, holding the glasses tilted just so. Mini loved the way he conducted himself. Rustom was a man of the world. Sophisticated, urbane, confident and on top of every situation. He raised his glass and she picked up hers to take a sip. He stopped her with a tap on her hand.

'We must look into each other's eyes when we toast. It makes the relationship stronger. Come on, look into my eyes,' he ordered, as he gazed at her.

Mini took a tentative sip, but Rustom tipped the glass and

swallowed every drop. He was in an especially exuberant mood, Mini could tell. After all, they had signed the biggest deal in the history of Soul Mates. She too was so proud to be part of it. Maybe she could move to Mumbai, she thought. She could find her own place, create a life for herself. She wouldn't miss Shyam for a minute. The only person she would miss was Polka. But she could make trips to Delhi and meet her. She would definitely be there for the delivery and to welcome her puppies. After that, she could settle down in Mumbai. She could just forget Sicko Shyam and start her own venture with Rustom. Of course, it would be strictly work, Mini assured herself.

Mini knew she was being tested. The path to true love was not paved with roses, she was aware. Didn't Samyukta and Prithviraj go through their trial by fire? Julia Roberts had to walk out on Richard Gere to make him realize what she meant to him. Sooner or later, somehow, Rustom would discover his love for her.

Rustom had finished the pitcher and had ordered another one. Mini switched to Diet Coke, not wanting to put on weight. Rustom was trim, so no worries of that sort for him. That was another aspect in Rustom that Mini really admired. He was so controlled about his diet, so regular at the gym. In fact, he was disciplined about everything. She had never seen him lose his cool, in spite of all the stress at work.

Sub-consciously, Mini had started comparing him with Shyam on every parameter. And so far, Shyam had lost out on each one. Looking at Rustom, so self-assured, masterful and handsome, Mini could feel her heart expand with love. Deepa would say it was lust. But Mini was going to prove her wrong.

There was a live band playing in the pub. Rustom bounded up to the stage, grabbed a mike and started singing out loud, his face flushed with merriment. It was an old Beatles number.

'I wanna hold your ha-a-a-and, I wanna hold your hand!' Rustom crooned, looking straight at her.

Mini blushed to the roots of her thinning hair. She looked around self-consciously. They were practically the only ones in the pub, the lull before office goers stormed it. Rustom whispered something in the pianist's ear. The Beatles faded out, making way for a dreamy, romantic melody. Mini couldn't take her eyes off Rustom. He was standing with his arms open wide, calling her across to dance with him. In a daze, Mini floated towards him, their eyes locked.

Neither of them noticed the door opening. A noisy group of people walked in. Rustom saw them first. They were the Soul Mates staff, from the creative, accounts and production departments. He dropped his arms and ran in the direction of the toilet. Mini was puzzled by his behaviour but didn't register anything till a pimply chap in a maroon jacket caught her in his arms and waltzed her around the pub. Mini tried to pull loose but the man had her in a clinch. To her horror, Mini realized that he was the head of Accounts. There were titters and sniggers all around. In the semi-darkness, Mini could make out other people from Soul Mates. She cast around desperately for Rustom but he had deserted her. Mini somehow extricated herself from the accountant's arms, grabbed her bag and beat a hasty retreat. As she left, she heard a comment that left her ears stinging.

'Looks like Lover Boy's left her in the lurch!' a voice said.

The answering retort was even more tasteless. 'Rustom sir is a real Chhupa Rustom!'

Mini was mortified. Was the whole office talking about her relationship with Rustom? It was so humiliating. And Rustom had shown her his true colours today. How dare he run away, leaving her to face the music? What a cad! Shyam would never

ever have done that, she was certain. He would have punched a few of those hecklers in their faces. In any case, what was the entire staff of Soul Mates doing in the pub? Had Rustom invited them for a celebration drink? The s.o.b. Obviously, she had got him all wrong. She was through with him. As soon as the wedding was over, she was leaving for home. Back to Shyam and Polka, where she belonged.

★ ★ ★

Mini reached Aditi's flat, hot, bothered and desperate for a drink. In her agitation, she reached out for Aditi's cigarettes and lit up. Opening the liquor cabinet, she poured herself a large whisky and gulped it in one go. She hadn't eaten much since the morning and the alcohol went straight to her head. Eyes swimming, she poured another stiff one and glugged it down. Her phone rang. Rustom's number flashed on the screen. She refused to take the call. He kept calling every two minutes but Mini was too angry to speak to him. The doorbell rang. A delivery boy stood there, holding a huge bouquet of blood-red roses. Mini was floored. For the first time in her life, someone had gifted her flowers, and that too, red roses. Rustom was a real charmer. But she was not going to forgive him, not just yet. Let him suffer for a while, Mini determined, her self-esteem rearing its head.

She was trying to decide which ice cream tub to order when Aditi came home, laden with chips, soda and beer.

'Hey, guess what!' she shouted happily. 'The gang is getting together tonight; they will all be here in an hour!'

Mini's mood soared. She hadn't met the girls since that disastrous night at Neelu's. 'Are they all coming?' she asked, slurring a bit.

'Dhira, Bhavna, Surekha ... aren't you happy? I can hardly wait!' Aditi exclaimed.

'Of course I am happy, I am verrry happy!' Mini said, tottering to the fridge for ice. And she *was* really happy. She loved the girls' gang, her very own sisterhood.

The Terrible Trio, Surekha, Dhira and Bhavna, arrived together. Mini was taken aback as they pounced on her collectively.

'Mini Mehta!' Bhavna screamed. 'What have you done to yourself? Looking so hot!'

Dhira stared at Mini's skirt. 'You've lost so much weight! Haven't seen you in a skirt since school!'

Surekha gave Mini the once-over and exclaimed, 'My my, Mini, who's the new man in your life?'

Dhira asked where Mini had got her 'smashing new' haircut. Mini was spared further interrogation by Aditi who came in with a tray with glasses and some ice. And by Bhavna, who had a diverting bit of news to share – Neelu, spokesperson and living specimen of the School of Perfect Marriage, was getting a divorce.

Dhira got up at once. She wanted to go meet Neelu and offer her the services of women-centric NGOs that she knew of. Bhavna was tickled pink. 'Dhira! Don't be so naïve. I'm sure this is just a publicity stunt. Too much black money. They are deflecting attention from their ill-gotten wealth, darling. They won't appreciate your intervention, trust me,' she said.

Surekha had another point of view. 'It's nazar. Someone who is jealous of Neelu had cast an evil eye on her.'

Dhira was puzzled. 'Evil eye? Who believes in that stuff anymore?'

'Boori nazar waaley tera muhn kaala!' said Mini. She had read that line on the backs of trucks on the Chandigarh highway. 'Ram ji ki fauj, karegi mauj,' she mumbled, remembering another such line. But she was beginning to feel guilty. She was jealous of Neelu, just a bit. Could she have willed Neelu's divorce? Was she turning into a frightful old black witch, killing marriages with a glance?

She asked Surekha to check her eyes. Surekha peered, pushed and prodded until a contact lens fell into Mini's drink. The sudden crisis succeeded in putting Neelu and her woes on the back-burner, as everyone joined in to rescue the lens. A strainer was brought from the kitchen. The whisky was poured into it and the lens was recovered. When Mini put it back in her eyes, it felt way more comfortable than before.

As the alcohol flowed, the evening took on a surreal feel. Surekha daintily picked up a glass of spiked orange juice and raised a toast. 'To Aditi, the only one among us who is not married,' she said.

Aditi raised her beer mug slowly. 'Come on girls, I'm just waiting for Mr Right.'

Dhira desultorily raised her rum and cola. 'Maybe you should look in an old-age home,' she remarked.

'Bitch,' replied Aditi.

Mini sat down and looked moodily into her fifth whisky. 'You know, one never stops looking for Mr Right.'

Aditi gave her a disbelieving look. 'Even after marriage?' she queried.

'Especially after marriage,' Mini said.

'That's crazy!' Dhira burst out.

Poor Dhira, she still thinks marriage is the be all and end all of life, Mini realized. 'Marriage is the end of romance.' Mini declared.

That got everyone thinking. Silence reigned till Bhavna sauntered across from the balcony to refill her glass. 'Girls! You'll never guess who I met! Pam!'

That got everyone keyed up. Pam had been the bad girl of the school, notorious for her utter disregard of rules and convention. 'Where?' they shrieked, in shrill unison.

'At the surgeon's,' Bhavna replied after a tantalizing pause. Surekha sniffed disdainfully and sat upright in her chair. She didn't like surgeons; her husband was one.

Bhavna leaned forward conspiratorially. 'Poor girl's been through a shocking tragedy!'

The others were hanging on to each word. She'd got them hooked. 'What happened?' they demanded to know.

Bhavna lowered her voice, playing to the gallery. 'That doctor who fixed her tummy…'

The suspense was killing the girls. They begged in unison. 'What? Tell!'

Bhavna took an aggravating sip from her glass, walked towards the girls and stopped dramatically in front of them. '… he botched it up!'

The girls ooh-ed and aah-ed at length. Bhavna bent low, bringing her lips close to the ears of the girls. 'Her belly button is now three inches lower!' she revealed with a flourish. The news was greeted by horrified shouts from all directions.

'Three inches lower? Meaning … oh my god!' Dhira spoke for them all.

The enormity of the botch-up hit them. There was silence for a while as they tried to digest the information.

'So … here's the moral of the story. Don't get a tummy tuck, unless you are planning to have an affair,' Bhavna said.

'I tried it. It's too tiresome,' Surekha said.

All heads turned to her. 'You? I don't believe you!' Bhavna exclaimed.

'You got a tummy tuck? Where from? How much did you pay?' Mini too jumped into the conversation, wanting all the details at once.

'No, not a tummy tuck! An affair,' Surekha replied.

The girls looked at her with sheer reverence. She had done what the rest had only thought about.

'Tell all, Surekha! Come on, no secrets in this room!' Dhira prodded.

'Well, if you must know ... this guy and I studied together in London. Years later, I bumped into him again in a jewellery shop and it turned out he owned it. We went out for coffee, got talking and found that we had a lot in common. Like, we had both abandoned our careers and put family first. We both loved diamonds. We missed London like crazy...' she continued wistfully.

Bhavna interrupted. 'Drop the mush, Surekha, come to the real stuff! Did you do it? How was it? Are you still seeing him?'

Dhira glared at Bhavna. 'Let her tell it in her own way,' she chided.

'That's all right, it was some time ago,' Surekha revealed with a world-weary sigh. 'It was hugely exciting to begin with, but all the lying and fibbing, and the fear of getting caught, I couldn't deal with the stress. I lost weight. My hair started falling. I had to invent a fictitious aunt, along with several fake girlfriends, even a false surname. Each time my phone beeped, I had a minor heart attack.'

A hush descended in the room. 'So how did it end?' Mini asked, breaking the silence.

'There was no future in the relationship. Just pain and panic. So I stopped meeting him. I had to block his number, bar his email. Much later I remembered that I had given him my most expensive diamond necklace to fix, but there was no way to get it back after the break-up,' Surekha said, tears rolling down her cheeks.

'Did he ever try to revive the relationship?' Bhavna wanted to know.

'I don't know, I didn't give him a chance,' Surekha replied.

'I have an idea,' Dhira said, slurring slowly. 'Let's all go to his shop and get the necklace back.'

'You mean, a robbery, with stockings on our heads? How exciting! Let's do it tonight!' Bhavna said, always ready for adventure.

'No, the necklace is not in the shop. I went for a family wedding last year and my aunt's daughter-in-law was wearing an identical necklace. I asked her where she got it from, and guess what? The bastard had sold it to her,' Surekha finished bitterly.

Bhavna gave Surekha a quick hug. 'I'm really sorry for your necklace, Surekha. I hope the asshole gets rocks in his kidneys,' she said with feeling.

Surekha nodded. 'Affairs are bad business, take it from me. Especially when it comes to women our age. We are rich and that makes us vulnerable to gold-diggers. So don't you girls do anything foolish … learn from my experience.'

Liquor loosened Mini's tongue. She drew her chair closer to Surekha's and spoke to her. 'Actually, I might just be having an affair, but there's no commerce involved in mine,' she said.

Aditi's eyes widened with interest. 'Now *this* is news,' she murmured.

'Really?' asked Dhira, wide-eyed. 'With whom?' she wanted to know.

'With Mr Right,' Mini replied.

Bhavna tossed back her drink and reached for another. 'And how, may I ask, do you know he's Mr Right? Isn't Shyam your Mr Right?'

'Two rights make a wrong, Mini,' Surekha said, sniffing disapprovingly.

Suddenly, everyone was glum. 'We are too old,' Bhavna said, sounding wistful.

Dhira sighed. 'I just discovered my first white hair', she said, running a hand through her locks.

'Who are you kidding, Dhira? We started graying long ago,' Bhavna retorted.

'I'm not talking about the hair on my head,' Dhira replied. Nobody said a word in response.

Mini leaned forward eagerly. 'Don't you see? That's why.'

'What are you talking about?' Aditi asked.

'I went to the gynae. Seems like I'll soon hit menopause. So if I don't have an affair now, it's going to be too late!' Mini explained.

'And Shyam? What about Shyam?' Aditi asked.

'What Shyam doesn't know can't hurt him,' said Mini, with a defensive shrug.

Dhira nodded vehemently. 'You're right! Now is the time. We are all the same age so … menopause will hit us at the same time…'

A loud shriek erupted from Aditi as she was hit by a terrible possibility. '*Girls*! I don't want to die a virgin!'

Dhira put a protective arm around her. 'We won't let you! What are friends for? I'm going to post your profile on lateshaadi.com.'

Aditi was aghast. 'Please, don't you dare do that. Plus, who's talking about marriage? I don't want to ever get married!'

Surekha had a suggestion. 'Is there a website for fuck buddies? Post her profile there,' she said.

'Mine too,' said Bhavna.

'Don't get into the heavy, emotional stuff, okay?' Dhira advised, fresh from a campaign on HIV Aids. 'No kinky business; only clean, healthy sex. And wear a condom.' She sounded like a school teacher.

'Sex is important, but what a girl needs is romance. What do you say, ladies?' Mini asked.

Aditi stood up and raised her glass. 'Hear, hear! I say let's all have affairs!'

Surekha went straight to the heart of the problem. 'But where are the men?'

Aditi was practically dancing with excitement by now. 'We'll hire them!' she shouted confidently.

Mini was appalled. 'Chhee! No way! We have to get them to fall for us!' she said, protesting.

'Even if it takes falsies!' said Aditi, looking down at her modestly endowed anatomy.

'Hey! Why don't we all go for a fuckation … er … a vacation?' Surekha suggested.

'Great idea! Let's! When?' Aditi cried, ready to leave on the next flight. Dhira was of the same mind.

'Now! We have no time to waste! Our body clocks are going tick-tock-tick-tock.' Aditi put her ear to Dhira's chest, earnestly trying to listen to the tick-tock.

'Count me out. I've got plans,' Mini's was the only dissenting voice.

'No way! We aren't going without you!' Aditi protested.

'But … I've got work. A great, big, royal wedding. And you know how Shyam is … he won't like it,' Mini protested.

'Leave Shyam to me. Get packing, girl,' Aditi insisted.

Bhavna and Dhira started circling the room, chanting 'tick-tock-tick-tock,' as Mini continued to remonstrate.

'I really can't make it this weekend. I *have* to be in Mumbai!'

'Why, Shyam's coming to town?' Aditi wanted to know.

'Tick-tock-tick-tock,' the chanting went on.

'No, it's work!' Mini cried.

'You're coming. That's it,' Aditi said, refusing to take 'no' for an answer. The 'Tick-tock-tick-tock' chant grew louder and more raucous. Aditi added a new line to it. 'Tick-tock-tick-tock. Bang-bang-to-Bangkok!'

Dhira started to slug Vodka straight from the bottle. A very tipsy Aditi put her arms around Mini and danced the waltz.

\* \* \*

Why was the sun so piercingly bright this morning? Mini groaned as her eyes squinted. A blinding headache made itself known as she stumbled towards the bathroom. Aditi was sitting at the dining table, nursing a huge mug of coffee.

'Hung-over? Me too,' she mumbled mournfully.

Mini shut herself in the bathroom, sinking down on the commode as a wave of nausea assailed her. She thought of taking the day off, but with the great royal wedding round the corner, there was no way she could. Dragging herself in and out of the shower, she got dressed and sat down for breakfast. One look at the bowl of porridge that Aditi put in front of her and she was back in the bathroom, retching. Never again, she thought. She was never ever going to drink again.

The coffee seemed to have helped Aditi. She looked pointedly at Mini and asked, 'What was all that last night, about having an affair? Don't you know Shyam is still crazy about you? Don't you do anything to hurt him, Mini. Such a romantic guy ... who would have thought our Shyam was a roses-and-chocolate man?' she demanded.

Mini wondered what she was talking about. Shyam had never sent her roses, not even when she was in hospital with gall-bladder stones. Aditi must be more drunk than she looked. Mini held her head between her palms and dizzily walked to the kitchen. Taking a spoonful of fruit salt, she poured a glass of chilled water and made herself swallow it. Within five minutes, she ought to feel ready to go, Mini thought, wincing at the kitchen bulb. Aditi had disappeared by the time she came back to the dining table. Sitting down, still clutching her head, Mini waited for the worst of the hangover to subside. She would go to work but she was not going to speak to Rustom. She would thank him politely for the flowers and keep to herself. If he behaved himself, maybe by the evening, she would think about acknowledging his existence.

The fruit salt started to work. Mini got up slowly and took baby steps towards the door. To her immense relief, the earth had stopped moving beneath her feet. She caught the sideboard for support and saw the flowers, now in full bloom. Her eyes fell on the attached card. It said, 'All is forgiven. Come back home. Shyam.'

* * *

The first thing Mini noticed on entering the office was how everybody stopped talking when they saw her. The next thing she noticed on her way to the water cooler, was a large picture on Rustom's desk. It showed a happy, smiling family – Rustom, his wife and a little boy.

Mini froze in dismay. Obviously, Rustom and she were the subject of office gossip. She was appalled. The Soul Mates grapevine was fast and furious. Before long, people in the Delhi office would get wind of her relationship with Rustom. She would be the laughing stock of Soul Mates. Rustom had been quick to take precautionary steps. Mini hurriedly took corrective measures of her own. She remembered the picture that Shyam had put into her suitcase before she left Delhi. Retrieving it from the bottom drawer of her desk, she placed it at an angle, in full view of everyone who cared to look. She followed that up with a gushing SMS to Shyam, thanking him for the roses. And to think she had almost thanked Rustom for them. As if Rustom cared enough to give her flowers. She should have known better, Mini scolded herself.

All day, Mini made it a point to tell her co-workers about the beautiful red roses her husband had sent her, taking special care to ensure that Sandra was within earshot. The whole office would know that her husband was crazy about her. Most of all, Rustom needed to get the message, Mini decided. She was not interested in men who ran away, leaving damsels in distress to their own devices. His behaviour in the pub that evening was inexcusable. And here she was thinking that he just might be *the one*. Mini sighed. She may as well face it. There was never going to be a Dream Lover in her life. Because Rustom had turned out to have feet of clay. Maybe God had recalled all dream lovers to his factory once he'd figured out that they were defective pieces.

# 6

Preparations for the wedding were in full swing. But Rustom and Mini refused to work together unless it was absolutely unavoidable. She stopped having lunch with him, carrying her food tray to the common lunch table instead. Seated there, she talked about how much her husband was missing her and how glad she would be when the wedding was over and she would be reunited with her family.

The situation was fast turning into a theatre of the absurd. Major decisions were being made without a word being exchanged. Mini stopped discussing things with Rustom and even scanned her signature so that she could give her approval on email. Rustom went a step further. He mailed still shots of dancers for the mehendi night, requesting her to approve the choreography.

But later that evening, there was simply nowhere to hide. When Mini got into the elevator, Rustom stepped in as the doors were closing. Mini stared in disbelief. The elevator descended jerkily, its creaking sound painfully loud in the silence. The tension became untenable. Mini couldn't stand it any more.

She burst out. 'So how are you, Turncoat?'

Rustom bristled. 'Speak for yourself, Madam. You are the one who has been running away from me.'

Mini was just about to deliver a biting retort when the elevator shuddered, swayed and came to a halt. The doors remained tightly shut.

Mini felt the familiar panic surging up. 'Oh my god! Why has the elevator stopped?' she squeaked in fright.

'It's probably a power cut,' Rustom replied, sounding amused.

Mini was furious. How could the man be so cocky after what he had done? 'At least this time you can't abandon me and run away,' Mini said cuttingly.

Rustom was quick to rise to his defense. 'I didn't abandon you. I was trying to save you,' he said.

Mini forgot her elevator phobia. She wasn't going to let Rustom get away with this. 'By leaving me alone with all those clowns?' she retorted.

Rustom was equally strident. 'What did you want me to do? Punch the hell out of them?'

'Yes, if you had any guts, you would have,' Mini shot back.

'And have one of them call our respective spouses? Gimme a break!' Rustom said bitterly.

Mini squirmed. Rustom was right. What could he have done, given the circumstances? But she wasn't fully appeased. 'At any rate, you should have done something,' she said.

'Maybe I should have acted like your lover? Or your husband?' Rustom bit out.

'Or a good friend,' Mini offered lamely. 'Ha! You think you and I can be "good friends"? Have you forgotten what happened the other night?' Rustom muttered.

Mini's heart did a cartwheel. No, she hadn't forgotten. But forgiveness was another matter altogether. 'Then why did you behave like I meant nothing to you? Like you didn't care?' Mini shot back.

'Do *you* care? What am I to you anyway? A toy boy? Someone to amuse yourself with while you are in Mumbai?' Rustom countered, sounding really annoyed.

'You know that's not true!' Mini quickly said.

'Prove it! Will you leave your beloved Shyam for me?' Rustom challenged. 'We'll go to Goa and live there ... start a new life.'

'Come on, Rustom, get serious,' Mini tried to lighten the situation.

'I've never been more serious,' Rustom replied, moving closer to Mini.

'How do I know you won't change your mind tomorrow?' Mini asked.

'Yeah ... how do I know you won't run back to Delhi tomorrow?' Rustom replied, coming closer, till Mini had her back to the elevator wall.

'I'm not the one who runs away, remember?' Mini said, looking up into Rustom's hazel eyes, her pulse racing.

'Is that a "no"? Or is it a disguised "yes"?' Rustom asked, leaning in, almost menacingly.

Mini couldn't move. Rustom's aggressive stance was making her uncomfortable. He leaned even closer, his lips hovering over hers. Mini panicked. 'No!! I mean, I don't know!' she cried out.

'See? How much you want from me and how closed you are!' Rustom said, placing one hand on either side of her on the elevator wall, effectively trapping her. Mini closed her eyes as his lips descended, her heart galloping like the swayamvar horses. Then his mouth covered hers and Mini was awash with delicious commotion.

They made a frenzied dash to the Soul Mates guest house.

Rustom was taking forever to find the door keys. Mini couldn't bear it and yanked open his shirt. She never could wait to tear the wrapping off gifts.

Falling on the bed, they went at each other like two hungry animals. Rustom tore at Mini's bra with his teeth. She bit at his shirt buttons. They clung together, like skin and bone. He nibbled, she nipped. He sucked, she bit. And when he had taken her again and again, Mini felt sated and complete.

\* \* \*

The wedding was upon them. So was the monsoon. Mini had never seen rain like this. It was relentless. The roads were oozing. Offices were shut for the day. Mini went into panic mode. There was so much to be done. They would never get the wedding off the ground. Aditi too had been forced to take the day off, but she didn't seem perturbed. Sitting in the balcony, she was sipping steaming mugs of tea and listening to Sufi qawwalis. Mini resigned herself to a day wasted. Even her phone signal was behaving badly. Picking up a book, she sat down to wait out the rain.

The music was distracting. It was heady, romantic stuff. Mini wondered why Sufi music was sung by men. The words were all about a woman's longing for her man.

'Jiska piya sang beetay sawan, us dulhan kee raein suhagan…'

Mini felt an uncontrollable pang of hunger. She grabbed a chocolate and got into bed. Soon she was lost in a fantasy where Rustom was down on his knees, softly serenading her as she stood in a high balcony. But when she slept, she dreamt that Rustom was slowly licking strawberry cream off her naked body.

\* \* \*

Shyam sat in the cane swing in the verandah of his home. Polka was due any day now. He wished Mini would come home. How could she do this to him, he cursed silently. She was smitten with that Parsi. He was familiar with the feeling. It was a midlife thing, a passing phase. He himself had gone through it years before, when he had fallen madly in lust with a yummy mummy at the tennis courts. Mini would soon come to her senses.

Shyam got up for a refill, pouring white rum into his glass and topping it with diet soda. He still hadn't recovered from the shock he'd received in Mumbai. Mini had changed. She had lost weight and was wearing make-up. She looked great. Not just the Parsi, the entire male population of the office must be lusting after her. Then why would she want her old, fat husband? When had his six-pack abs become six packs of flab? Immediately on his return from Mumbai, he had joined the gym and switched to white rum. Getting back into shape was an uphill battle. But he wasn't giving up.

When had things started to go wrong? Shyam tried to figure out. Mini and he had been through so much together. Was she now going to let his paunch come between them? Mini was his wife, he needed her. There was no way he was going to lose her. Not to that effeminate Parsi. Not to any other man. Shyam raised a belligerent toast to the thought and downed the glass.

\* \* \*

Wedding panic assumed critical mass over the week. Murphy's Law was running riot. This morning it was the wedding guests who were acting up.

The royal guests had started to arrive. Soul Mates had booked rooms in every hotel in town. The groom's father had furnished a list of invitees. There was strict protocol to be followed. Immediate family was to stay in suites in five-star hotels, first and second cousins were booked into deluxe rooms while third, fourth and fifth cousins were in standard rooms in three-star properties. But all hell broke loose when an erstwhile raja of a minor principality arrived and demanded the Presidential suite of the hotel he was booked into. The hotel called Rustom.

Mini had just stepped into Rustom's cabin and was admiring his chiselled profile, when the call came. Rustom cursed, spluttered and sighed.

'These bloody kings! Somebody ought to tell them that their privy purses are empty,' he said.

'Thus spake the king of hearts,' Mini murmured inadvertently.

Rustom grinned. 'And do I occupy the Presidential suite in your heart, my lady?'

Mini batted her eyelashes. 'Oh no, that is reserved for my Prince Charming. He's going to come on a black charger and sweep me off my feet.'

Rustom's phone rang. It was the hotel again. Rustom got to his feet and barked. 'Sandra! Call the office car to the porch. Now!'

Mini stood up too. 'What happened? Can I come along?' Rustom rushed out without replying. Mini picked up her bag and followed.

Apparently there was pandemonium at the hotel. The minor Raja was threatening to boycott the wedding if he was not given his suite. The groom's party was panicking as the only Presidential suite in the hotel was occupied. Something had to be done.

Mini caught herself wondering what she was doing in the car. It was not her job to fix hotel rooms. A sneaky voice inside told her that she was there only to be with Rustom, hoping to get him alone in one of the hotel rooms. Immediately, the prude in her tried to justify her behaviour. As a senior Soul Mates employee, every crisis the company faced was her problem as well. But her conscience wasn't buying the argument. Because deep down, she knew she was there only to help Rustom out of a scrape. Mini sat up, straight and defiant. If helping the man she loved was a crime, well then, she was guilty as charged.

★ ★ ★

The harassed manager on duty took one look at Rustom and sagged with relief.

'So glad you came, Sir,' he gushed as he led them to his office. 'The Presidential suite, Sir, is already occupied by the prince's maternal uncle. I've offered the raja our Viceroy suite but he has point blank refused,' he explained, wiping his brow. 'He's sitting in his Rolls-Royce in the porch. Just now he sent word that if the suite is not made available to him in the next five minutes, he will start to unpack in the lobby,' he continued. 'You will appreciate, Sir, this is royalty, and I don't want to tread on any er ... blue-blooded toes,' he finished breathlessly.

Rustom sighed. He asked the manager to check with other hotels if they had a Presidential suite available. There were none. Then Mini had a brainwave.

'Just switch the nameplates. Put the Presidential suite nameplate on the Viceroy suite and vice versa. He will never know.'

Rustom and the manager looked at her in awe. 'What an idea, Mrinaliniji, what an idea!' Rustom exclaimed, chuffing Mini on the back.

The manager however, was not fully convinced. 'We can't do that, sir. That would amount to fraud. The repercussions could be huge,' he said, a trifle snootily.

Mini sighed. The world was full of unimaginative, stuffed-shirted morons. She looked at Rustom. He winked and rapidly punched a number into his mobile. Mini could tell he was speaking to a fellow Parsi. He finished talking and handed the phone to the manager. Mini watched the manager's face turn pale as he nodded furiously. Ashen-faced, he ended the conversation and addressed Rustom. 'Sir, it's an excellent idea, but ... can it be our little secret? I don't want word to get out; it could become embarrassing if the press got to know. Unfavourable publicity and all that...' he said apologetically.

A triumphant Rustom led Mini back to the car. Mini was bursting with curiosity. 'Who did you speak to? It worked like magic,' she said. Rustom spoke with a swagger in his voice. 'To my uncle. He is on the hotel board.'

Mini was impressed. Rustom was flushed with triumph. 'That twit of a manager thinks he is so smart. I put him in his place. He doesn't know how powerful I am. In fact, I'm going to speak to my uncle and get the bugger sacked!'

Mini was aghast. 'You can't do that! The chap was just doing his job!' she exclaimed.

'Then he should have managed things better. His behaviour wasn't professional,' Rustom said.

'I don't think he was unprofessional. He was just in a difficult situation, that's all,' Mini protested.

'You're being too soft, Mini. This is a cut-throat world ... perform or perish,' Rustom said, with a sneer.

'And walk all over people on your way up?' Mini asked.

'Heard the one about the girl who climbed the ladder, lad by lad?' Rustom said, suddenly becoming playful.

Mini laughed, but she was filled with disquiet. This was a side of Rustom she had not seen before this. She was silent on the drive back to the office. Mini had a highly developed sense of justice and fancied herself a champion of the underdog. The front-office chap at the hotel wasn't really to blame, she thought. Of course, as a graduate from the School for Stuffed Shirts, the man deserved the third degree. On the other hand, he probably had an ailing mother and seven hungry children to feed. But the really disturbing aspect in the whole episode was Rustom's attitude. Real men didn't pick on people who couldn't fight back.

She found herself thinking of the time when Shyam's father's driver had been caught taking the new car to his son's wedding, on the pretext of taking it for wax polishing. The neighbour's cook had spilled the beans. Shyam had been incensed to begin with. But after the driver told them his 'izzat' had been at stake, he had let him borrow the car for all the ceremonies, right up to the bidai. The driver became Shyam's most loyal champion, a slave for life.

Mini was filled with a grudging disquiet. In her mind, Rustom was the perfect gentleman – kind, chivalrous and proper. Had she discovered a chink in his armour? She was over-reacting, Mini decided and pushed the episode to the back of her mind.

* * *

Shyam had a date with the gynaecologist. He carefully bundled Polka into the car and drove to the ultrasound clinic. The evening before, the vet had seen signs of foetal distress and Shyam was not taking any chances.

To his dismay, he was the only father in the clinic's maternity ward. All the other girls were accompanied by their mothers. Polka whimpered as she was lifted up to the gynaecologist's table. On the adjacent table, an attractive female was crooning to a dachshund with a swollen tummy. Shyam cursed Mini. She should be here to take care of Polka, he thought.

The female smiled sympathetically at Shyam. 'First-time daddy?' she enquired.

Shyam grimaced. 'Yes. Wife's travelling, so...'

The woman's eyes widened with sympathy. 'Aww! Poor baby!' she said, lavishing attention on Polka. 'Don't worry, Daddy will take good care of you!' she warbled.

Shyam beamed at her. He was loopy about dogs and instantly warmed up to those who shared his obsession. 'When are you due?' he enquired.

The lady gave him a coy look. 'We'll know after the ultrasound, won't we, Muffin?'

'So will I,' Shyam replied grimly.

An attendant came and started to apply some white gook on Polka's stomach. Polka shivered but lay acquiescent. But Muffin refused to take things lying down. When it was her turn for the gook application, she growled menacingly. When that didn't work, she tried to leap off the table and bite the attendant. The pretty female shrieked. Shyam rushed to the rescue.

The moment he left Polka's side, she let out a loud howl. It seemed to be infectious, as dog after dog added their voice to the cacophony, till even the stray dogs on the street outside seemed to have caught on. Muffin, meanwhile, had run amok. It was pandemonium for a bit, till two attendants caught hold of Muffin and muzzled her.

Thereafter the ultrasound proceeded at a fast clip. The vet

shared his opinion with Shyam. 'She's healthy, and there are at least a dozen pups in there. Delivery could happen any time.'

Shyam swelled with pride. Twelve pups! It would be a hoot, he thought, as he picked up Polka and headed towards the car.

He had just settled Polka down and was reversing out when Muffin and the female came out.

'So what's the due date?' Shyam yelled out.

The female forlornly wiped a tear. 'There won't be any pups. There were two, but they are stillborn,' she said, choking on a sob.

Shyam's euphoria waned. Rushing to Muffin's side, he reached out to give her a hug. She snapped. Shyam yelped. Blood dripped. The female screamed. She snatched Muffin and dumped her into the car. Shyam trooped back to the clinic to get a tetanus shot, the female following two steps behind, apologizing frantically. She insisted on exchanging phone numbers so that she could make sure that Shyam's hand was healing well.

* * *

A crisis. A beautiful, full-blown crisis! Mini just loved it. A crazy, meaty work problem got her creative juices flowing like nothing else.

It was Laveena, the bride, who called Mini. They had met on several occasions and she had taken a shine to Mini. Mini too liked her rather bold and bohemian outlook to life. But nothing had prepared Mini for the shocker she now unleashed.

Laveena wanted to call off the wedding.

Mini called Rustom. Rustom called the groom's father. The groom's father called the groom. The groom called Laveena who called Mini, placing the crisis squarely in Mini's lap. Mini arranged to meet Laveena to discuss the situation. All hopes were pinned on her. If the wedding got cancelled, Rustom would lose his job. The groom's father would lose face. The groom would lose it. Mini had to win.

They sat in Laveena's vanity van in Film City, where Laveena was shooting for a Bhojpuri film. Her hairdresser and make-up man were readying her for the next shot, applying highlights to her cheeks and hair. Mini tried to talk over the hum of the hairdryer.

She broached the subject. 'So what on earth happened, Laveena? You were going to marry your Prince Charming! How could you call it off? Did you have a fight, did the prince say something?'

Laveena batted her false eyelashes. 'Oh no, nothing like that, the prince didn't do anything,' she sighed. 'All I did was ask for a pre-nup agreement. They got cold feet. That's all,' she said, yawning.

Mini was aghast. 'I thought you were in love! Isn't that enough?' she asked.

Laveena tittered. 'Grow up, Mini! Love won't feed me when I'm forty and the prince has forty mistresses. On the other hand, forty crores would be enough, at least for a while,' Laveena drawled, as she gazed into the mirror, flicking away a bit of lint from her lip.

'But you really seemed to be into the prince. I thought you couldn't wait to get married,' Mini protested weakly.

'Sure, I thoroughly enjoyed shopping for the wedding! Clothes, jewellery, shoes, bags ... never had so much fun in my life! Especially that trip to Dubai to buy gold ... that was a high point ... what an experience!' she exclaimed.

Mini felt thoroughly dejected. 'And here I thought I was planning the ultimate fairytale wedding,' she muttered in despair.

'Darling, all I've ever wanted was to marry a man with a no-limit expense card. Get the prince to agree to a pre-nup and this fairytale could end happily ever after,' Laveena sighed dreamily.

A sober Mini promised to talk to the prince. As the car sped back to the office, Mini brooded over the situation. Why was the world so cynical, she rued. Soon, she told herself, she would be the only person on planet Earth who believed in old-fashioned love and romance. Or could it be that it was she who was the deluded one? Maybe there really wasn't a perfect relationship, maybe men and women could never actually be soulmates. Maybe God had devised love as a trick to make people have sex and he had made sex only to populate the world, she pondered glumly. She thought of Rustom and gave herself a shake. There was no cause for disillusionment. What she felt for Rustom was true love, barring the few instances of lust which Mini liked to believe, were an aberration she intended to correct. Given time, Rustom would respond to her with true love. This story was going to get its happily-ever-after ending.

Hectic parleys saw the groom's father capitulating. A prenuptial agreement was drawn up. It went on to become a reference point in all high society weddings thereon, largely because of the Rottweiler clause.

In the event of a divorce, Laveena wanted the prince's Mumbai penthouse to move to her. She also demanded a luxury yacht in case the prince had an extramarital affair. But the prince had a trump card that Laveena hadn't reckoned with. He got a clause added whereby his pet rottweiler dogs would have sleeping rights in the couple's bedroom suite. Laveena pleaded, wept and argued, but the prince stuck to his guns. Finally,

Laveena dropped the penthouse and the prince dropped the Rottweiler clause.

The lawyers had the last laugh, the pre-nup was signed and Soul Mates was back in business. But Mini was furious. Polka often shared the bed with Shyam and her and they loved it. Now Laveena was depriving the prince and his pets of the pleasure. Mini was all set to report the matter to the Mumbai Dog Lovers Club, but Rustom wouldn't hear of it. Shyam would have understood, Mini thought unhappily.

# 7

The day of the wedding dawned. Mini would never ever forget the experience. She had never laughed so much in her whole life. Or cried so hard.

Everything went smoothly till it was time for the wedding procession to roll out. The groom left for the swayamvar in a limousine with insignia emblazoned and flags aflutter. The rest of the procession assembled a short distance from the venue and re-grouped in royal style to herald the prince's arrival.

The procession began with full fanfare. At the head were a dozen majestic horses with nagara players seated on their backs. Behind them were young retainers of the family, riding horses, sporting turbans and swords. Following them was the prince himself, atop a gaily caparisoned elephant.

Mini and Rustom were in an open jeep, a few hundred yards ahead of them all, keeping an eye on the procession's progress. Mahatta had arrived the previous night and had lavished praise on Mini, loudly proclaiming his appreciation for her hard work. He drove alongside in his hired car, leading from the front, as overall boss. His presence was making Rustom tense. He was compulsively barking orders into his walkie-talkie every few seconds. Mini was excited and happy, waiting for the swayamvar to start. She gazed at the sky, her face glowing, as beautiful fireworks showered multi-coloured sparks.

It was probably a spark that started it. Just as the procession entered the resort's gates, the elephant carrying the groom went berserk.

The prince had to jump off to save his hide. But it was a case of from-the-frying-pan-into-the-fire. He landed in a cactus bush. The elephant rushed at the welcome gate erected in the prince's honour and decimated it. Trampling through the resort's manicured hedges, it burst upon the lawn where the guests were savouring starters and cocktails. There was utter chaos. Then he changed track and charged towards the parking lot where it flipped over cars. An unsuspecting Rolls-Royce arrived at the gate and blew the horn. The elephant paused, roared in rage and sent it hurtling into a roadside ditch, the driver leaping out just in time. Rustom frantically called for security.

When the hotel authorities realized that the elephant was out of control, they called the forest officials who rushed a wildlife NGO to the rescue. A team of trigger-happy officials marched determinedly in the direction of the elephant, armed with tranquillizing darts. Darts flew, people ran helter-skelter. Luckily, one of them found its mark and soon the elephant was brought under control.

Meanwhile, Mahatta, who had a propensity to go in the bushes, got a dart in his rump and dropped unceremoniously at the groom's maternal aunt's feet.

Mini stared, stupefied. Her worst nightmare was coming true. She cursed herself for not putting her foot down. She had protested against the elephant, as there was already a chariot for the prince. Besides, he was going to use his personal stallion for the swayamvar. But the groom's father had had his way. Now, nothing was going according to plan.

The prince was to disembark at the porch and then move in the chariot to the swayamvar venue. But the elephant had turned the dignified royal procession into a Chaplinesque farce. The Siamese cats had run amok and the trainer was running around making strange cat calls. Mini tottered into the hotel, moved to the bar and downed a large one and followed it up with another. The world righted itself. As the whisky blunted the elephant's impact, Mini felt her crisis management skills sharpen.

Her walkie-talkie crackled. It was a panicked Rustom, summoning her to the swayamvar pavilion. Mini rose from the bar stool and leapt to the rescue. Thereafter, everything went smoothly, except for a snorting horse or two. The only serious casualty was Mahatta, who roamed around with a cushion held to his posterior.

The swayamvar itself was magnificent and Mini found herself wiping her eyes as the prince whisked away the starlet. It was a striking picture, right up there with the last scene from *Pretty Woman* and *Dilwale Dulhania Le Jaayenge*. Mini was awash with feelings of loss. She had pinned so many hopes on her own marriage and it had been the big disenchantment of her life.

Standing there, neck deep in romantic vibes, Mini had a private pity party. She thought of how things could have been if she had met Rustom earlier, before they had got married to their respective spouses. She mourned for all the missed sunsets, the unsung serenades and the aborted candlelit dinners. But at least she had met Rustom, her Dream Lover. How many people were so lucky, Mini consoled herself. Life had given her a chance to rewrite her romantic history. She was going to grab it.

* * *

It hit Mini like a tonne of bricks. She woke up the morning after with a serious realization. Perhaps it was the release of so much pent-up anxiety over the wedding or maybe she was just exhausted but Mini didn't feel like getting out of bed in the morning.

Actually, it was neither. It was the thought of parting from Rustom that was making Mini miserable. The great, royal wedding was over. She was overstaying her welcome in Mumbai.

So was this it, Mini thought. The beginning and end of romance in her life. Mission incomplete. Abort, abandon and revert to status quo. It was all so confusing. She had made her feelings for Rustom very clear to him, but she still couldn't bank on his. Sometimes he seemed to reciprocate. At other times, he was indifferent. Was the wheelchair impeding him? Was it a moral dilemma? As for herself, she didn't even have to think. If she had to choose between Shyam and Rustom, Rustom won hands down.

She was in love with a man who hadn't said he loved her. What would happen next? Well, she had been married to predictability most of her life. It was time for a change, Mini decided bleakly.

\* \* \*

The office had a pleasant languor about it. Like the lull after the squall. The staff sauntered in at a deliciously late 11.00 a.m., for once not rushing to meet a deadline. The great, royal wedding was over. There was a gap before the next project's mayhem began.

She walked into her cabin, feeling at a complete loss. She was not part of the next project. There was nothing to do. Gloom descended. Moodily, she switched on her computer. *Ping!* Deepa was online, from the Delhi office. Obviously, she would want to know when Mini would be back. Mini ignored her and started a game of Spider Solitaire. She could hear Rustom talking on the phone in his cabin. Should she go up to him, find out what his intentions towards her were? Or should she wait for him to make the move? When you flee, they follow and when you follow, they flee. There was always a grain of truth in old jungle sayings of this nature. Mini sat down to bide her time.

★ ★ ★

Rustom was in his cabin, going through the wedding pictures uploaded by the office photographer. He came across a picture of himself. Not bad, he thought smugly. He could still set a few hearts aquiver. Certainly one particular lady, sitting in the next cabin, was completely besotted. He clicked through a few more pictures. There was one of the bridegroom galloping away with the bride. In the very next shot, the photographer had captured Mini, naked longing on her face, as she watched the horse disappear into the sea mist.

It was time to make his next move. Rustom lifted the phone and punched in a number. 'Gomes? How are you? I'll be coming down this weekend, with a special friend. I want you to arrange for a horse. Yes, I said "horse". Got it? Do it.'

He disconnected and called Mini's cabin. 'Hi, Sexy. If you're free, come and have a look at the wedding pictures,' he said. Putting the phone down, Rustom smiled in amusement. What a talented woman, he mused. And so unaware of her own worth. She would be priceless as a partner, in every sense of the term. The royal wedding project had consolidated Rustom's stock in the market and his financier was more than ready to back him. Now all that remained was to persuade Ms Mini. Maybe he could offer Mahatta a job then, he thought, his mind turning to his rotund boss, occupying the conference room that very moment.

He smiled as Mini walked in and patted the chair next to his, tilting the computer screen at an angle so that they could view the wedding pictures together. 'Best wedding show this company's ever put up,' he commented, as they gazed at a picture of the horses marching regally down the road. 'Most people thought we had planned the elephant riot, just to spice things up.'

Mini perked up. Rustom always had this effect on her. She could be down in the dumps but one word from him could make her heart soar. All the same, Mini couldn't shake off the despair that was engulfing her. 'But good thing it's over,' she muttered. 'Now I can go back home to my life. It's been a good break but...'

Rustom picked up the cue. 'Talking of breaks, I could use one right now. Why don't we go to Goa?'

Mini's heart did a trapeze swing. 'I would love to,' she exclaimed, all her resolutions melting before the heat in Rustom's gaze.

'I have a secret den there. No one knows about it,' Rustom murmured.

'We could stay there and save on hotel costs,' Mini said, blushing.

'It's got a tiny, secluded beach. You can sunbathe in private,' Rustom whispered wickedly.

'With you looking on?' Mini said, rather alarmed.

'Wouldn't miss it for the world,' Rustom mock-leered.

'I don't know if it's such a good idea,' said Mini. Her mind raced. Could there possibly be enough time to get her stretch marks lasered? She kicked herself for not doing the tummy tuck when there was time.

'Why not? It will be you, me, sun, sand, waves … we can talk all day, laze, make sand castles … and at night…' Rustom continued.

'And at night?' Mini asked, breathless. Rustom grinned wolfishly and placed his hand on her thigh. Hugely embarrassed, Mini pretended to examine the photograph on the screen. It was the elephant, running roughshod in the hotel garden, uprooting a Masanda bush.

The intercom rang. Rustom answered. 'Hello? Yes Sir, she is here. Just a minute.' He looked at Mini who had a stricken expression on her face. 'Boss wants to speak to you right away,' he said.

Mini went off without a word, her heart plummeting. She knew what was coming. Mahatta was going to deport her back to Delhi.

Ten minutes later, Mini emerged tearfully from the conference room and crept back to Rustom. 'I want to drive down but flying will save time,' he said, glancing up from his computer screen as Mini entered.

'I'm not going,' a miserable Mini said in a crushed voice.

'Why? What's wrong? Don't tell me you're chickening out,' Rustom protested.

'Boss wants me to head back to Delhi ASAP. The wedding is over … no need for me to stay on,' Mini replied tersely.

'Give me a minute. Let me speak to the boss', Rustom said as he disappeared into Mahatta's temporary office in the conference room.

Mini sat there, distraught, looking at the screen where the wedding pictures were displayed. There was one of her, looking anxious, lost in thought. She checked another picture. It was Rustom, drink in hand, looking heartbreakingly handsome. Good enough to eat, thought Mini, the tears threatening to flow again.

Rustom came back to the room. 'That's settled then,' he said.

'What is?' Mini queried, still nursing that end-of-the-world feeling.

'We have decided to give you a farewell. Since half the staff is not in today, it will be on Monday. We will leave for Goa this evening and be back in time for the farewell,' he said.

Mini looked at him with unadulterated worship in her eyes. What a masterful man, she thought, and he wanted to whisk little old Mini away to his private den in Goa. Who would have thought, she asked herself in wonder. The man did love her. The confession would come in Goa, she hoped.

Mini put up a token protest. 'Uh, I need to think about this.' She said.

Rustom looked deep into her eyes, putting his hand on hers. 'You still need to think?' Mini felt her heart melt and puddle up in a mush. She was about to curl her fingers around Rustom's when her phone rang.

'Hello? Shyam? … Oh it went off really well … When? … Oh. Really? That's … that's wonderful … Tomorrow? … Yes, the work is over, but … of course I love her! What do you mean? … But my farewell is on Monday. I have to attend my own send-off, don't you think? … But it looks so rude! How can I leave without attending it? … You've sent it? … No, I haven't got it. I'll call you a little later, okay? Bye.'

'Your husband?' Rustom asked.

'I don't think I can go to Goa,' Mini replied. 'I need to be back home tomorrow. Polka, our Golden Retriever, is about to deliver pups, any moment now,' she explained.

But Rustom was not about to be shaken off so easily. He looked deep into Mini's eyes and spoke. 'I don't care. You're coming. And that's final.'

Mini shook her head. 'But what about Polka? This is her first time! I must be there for her!'

'And what about us? Don't we deserve our time together?' he asked.

Mini gave in. 'Okay, but on Monday I must go,' she replied.

'We'll worry about Monday on Monday,' Rustom said triumphantly.

The office boy came with an envelope for Mini. She opened it to find her return ticket to Delhi, sent by Shyam. What was with Shyam, Mini thought irritably. The office would book her ticket, what was the need for him to act so efficient? She would just have to get it postponed to Monday, Mini figured. But how could she abandon Polka? On the other hand, birthing was a natural process and animals instinctively knew what to do under the circumstances. But if she went back to Delhi now, she would be throwing away her secret fantasies to the winds. Mini was on the horns of a dilemma.

The horny side won.

\* \* \*

In the evening, Mini went to Aditi's flat and packed her suitcase. She would go to Goa and fly to Delhi directly from there. The farewell would be a bore anyway, might as well give it a miss, Mini figured.

She was putting her clothes in the suitcase when her phone pinged. It was a text message from Shyam. Strange, Mini thought. Shyam hated texting. He didn't have the patience for it and ended up making a hilarious faux pas. Once, he had sent new year greetings to his entire phone list, except that he had typed 'Happy Nude Mother'.

Smiling, Mini glanced at the message and froze.

'Polka is in labour. If you not back on time, I'll be filing for divorce,' it read.

Divorce?

Shyam wanted to end the marriage? He was serious, Mini realized. She was too stunned to respond. The likelihood of divorce hadn't occurred to Mini so far, not seriously at least. In the sense that while she had often thought of divorcing Shyam, it hadn't occurred to her that Shyam may be the one to sever ties. That possibility had never crossed Mini's mind.

Did Shyam mean it? Mini sat down heavily and poured herself a single malt. It was a sobering realization. Real life had intruded upon her private fantasy with Rustom. Was she about to throw away a lifetime of marriage for a weekend in Goa?

Mini was full of confusion. What if she left Shyam? Would Rustom leave the wheelchair for her? How would life be without the solid comfort of marriage? What Rustom was offering her was very enticing, like a sinful dessert. But marriage was like daal-roti; essential for survival. A woman couldn't stay alive on dessert alone, Mini's mind reasoned. Plus it wasn't as if she had a future with Rustom. He too had his daal-roti to contend with.

Nervous and shaken, Mini felt the tears forming in her eyes, for the nth time that day. The heavens were conspiring against her, she thought wretchedly. Why else would Polka choose to deliver just as she was about to realize her lifelong dream? Life was so unfair.

Mini admonished herself. How could she think of herself when Polka needed her? She had to rush to her side. That was all that mattered, Mini decided. She would go back to Delhi. And if love was meant to happen, it would happen naturally. If Rustom loved her, he would come after her.

She glanced at her phone. If she left right away, she would beat the rush-hour traffic. She wheeled her suitcase out into the corridor and had just inserted the key into the lock when the single malt sloshed in her nether regions.

She was in the loo when the doorbell rang. It must be the building caretaker, Mini figured, who had come to take the keys.

Mini came out of the loo. She turned the door handle. Nothing budged. She was locked into the flat. The caretaker must have seen the keys in the lock, rung the bell, decided she had left and locked up when she didn't respond. She would have to clamber down from the balcony. Luckily, Aditi's flat was not too high up and the drop was manageable.

She had just put one gingerly foot on the railing when a roar filled her ears. She looked up and saw an apparition. It was déjà vu. Goosebumps erupted on Mini's flesh; a man was sitting astride a black motorbike, waving at her.

Mini pinched herself. No, it was not an alcohol-induced hallucination. This was for real. It was the very scene she had seen in her dreams all her life. Even the swayamvar was just a variation of the same theme. Only now, she was the protagonist and this was her lover. Her heart thudded as the man removed his helmet. Yes, it was Rustom.

Her knight had finally arrived to save her from her dreary existence. He came closer, stopped right below the balcony, handed her an envelope and sped away.

When Mini's heart stopped thudding, she opened the envelope that Rustom had carried to her. It was the print-out of a ticket to Goa. The flight was for the same evening.

As the taxi sped to the airport, Mini tried to think how she was going to tell Shyam that she was not returning to Delhi till Monday. Because after the balcony scene she had just been a part of, there was no doubt in her mind. Rustom was Dream Lover. She would go to Goa. It was destined.

★ ★ ★

Mini stood in the long queue before the luggage X-ray machine, lost in her thoughts. What if Shyam actually filed for divorce? Could a man really divorce his wife because she could not be there for their dog's delivery? Why was Shyam behaving in such an uncharacteristic manner? Could he have found out about Rustom?

Someone tapped her shoulder. 'Which flight are you on?' an elderly woman behind her enquired. 'Delhi ... er ... Goa...' Mini replied, flustered.

'You don't know where you are going?' the lady asked, puzzled.

'No, I don't, not that it's any of your business!' Mini replied rudely.

'I was just wondering, if by chance we are on the same flight, you could, perhaps, help me...' the lady replied, taken aback.

'Sorry,' Mini said gruffly, as she placed her luggage in the X-ray machine. Collecting it from the other end, she rushed to the loo again. Her digestive system invariably acted up whenever she was nervous, and she hadn't been this nervous in the longest time.

★ ★ ★

Shyam sat in front of the television, furious. Mini was not taking his calls or replying to his SMS. Polka was wandering around the room restlessly, whining mournfully every now and then. Shyam tried to control his panic. According to the vet, childbirth didn't need assistance or intervention. Shyam wished he could believe that.

He switched on the television but was so anxious, even Gambhir's batting couldn't distract him. Unable to relax, he paced up and down the corridor, glancing at his phone, willing it to ring. Suddenly, it did, and Shyam almost jumped out of his skin. But the number that flashed was not Mini's.

Shyam answered and a honey-sweet voice filled his ear. 'Hello? Have the darlings arrived yet?' the person trilled. 'This is Muffin's mommy, remember me?'

Shyam did remember her. It was the female from the vet's. What a blessing, Shyam thought gratefully. 'No, but any moment now,' he replied.

'Need assistance in production?' she wanted to know.

Shyam gave her directions to the house and let out a huge sigh of relief.

★ ★ ★

There was still time. Neither of the two flights had been called out as yet. Mini's mind was spaghetti and her stomach was soup.

The lady from the X-ray queue sat down next to her. 'They haven't opened the counter yet. I guess I am too early,' she muttered. She glanced up at Mini's pale face. 'Are you all right, beta?'

Mini felt tears prickling the back of her eyes. Sympathy always made her teary. 'I'm … a little unwell,' she replied.

The older lady sighed. 'Everybody's got troubles,' she said perceptively.

'I can't make up mind where to go. A friend wants me to spend the weekend with her. My husband wants me back home,' she lied.

'And what do *you* want?' the lady asked softly.

'I don't know. Er ... excuse me...' Mini rushed to the loo once again.

★ ★ ★

Rustom had taken the earlier flight to Goa, wanting to prepare for Mini's arrival. He poured himself a drink. Mini will be here soon, he thought, smiling with anticipation. The evening ahead was very important for him. There was a lot at stake, he knew. Mini was not one of his usual floozies; he cared for her. Life was so unfair, he thought. If he was rich, he wouldn't need Nilufer's dad to finance his business. But having taken her father's money, he had tied himself inextricably to Nilufer. He simply couldn't afford Mini. But in his heart and with his body, he could be true to Mini. And that was what he would do. He needed her.

★ ★ ★

Mini came back to the lobby and sat down weakly next to the kind woman. Her phone rang. She fumbled hurriedly in her bag. 'Sicko' flashed on the screen. She disconnected.

The older woman glanced at her. 'Is that your husband or your ... friend?' she enquired softly.

'Neither. It's a bank loan agent,' Mini replied. 'So ... where are you going?' she asked, quickly blocking more questions.

'Back home. Came to Mumbai to meet my daughter and her family. Now looking forward to my home and husband.'

'How long have you been married?' Mini asked.

'Sixty years!' the lady answered proudly.

'Sixty years! To the same man?' Mini exclaimed.

'Yes, of course,' the lady replied indignantly.

There was a sudden flurry in the airport lobby as a Bollywood actress arrived. Airline officials whisked her away to the VIP lounge as streams of fans chased behind.

'Isn't that the actress, Shailaja Kumari?' The forever-married lady asked.

'Yes it is … her divorce is all over the papers. Very messy…' Mini said, looking around distractedly.

'Why get married if you are going to get divorced?' The forever-married lady wondered aloud.

Mini swallowed nervously. 'Maybe she fell out of love with her husband?' she offered tremulously.

The lady sighed. 'Love? Love doesn't just happen. It has to be worked upon over a lifetime. Because before love, comes respect and before respect, understanding…' she rambled on. 'And this is where women go wrong.'

'Er … yes, of course … you are so right,' Mini agreed lamely.

'But you don't make the same mistake, okay?' the lady gently said.

Mini's mind went into a tizzy. Was she inviting her own ruin? Would she become an unglorified Shailaja Kumari, a desperate, sexually-abused drug addict on the decline? Rustom had never spoken about marriage. What would happen after Goa? Her feverish brain threw up dreary possibilities. Shyam would divorce her. Rustom would go back to Wheelchair. And she herself would be left with nowhere to go. It was a moment of cold clarity. Chills ran down her spine.

Turning to the forever-married lady, she said, 'Yes, I've decided, I'm going home.'

* * *

The airline opened its Delhi check-in counter. A sadder but wiser Mini walked up and joined the queue, the forever-married lady following closely. Mini was going to Delhi, no two ways about it. What could she be thinking, going all the way to Goa for a roll in the hay? Deserting Polka in her hour of need? How could she?

She called Rustom's number. He picked up on the first ring. Mini spoke in an urgent whisper, aware that the forever-married lady was all ears. 'Hello? Rustom?'

Rustom's familiar voice floated into Mini's ears like forbidden fruit. 'Mini, I'm waiting ... when are you going to be here?' he enquired eagerly.

'Rustom, I'm going home,' Mini said quietly, her heart diving into her shoes.

'Home? Did you say home? But I am not at home, I am in Goa, waiting for you!' Rustom sounded alarmed.

A hysterical laugh threatened to escape from Mini's mouth. 'I'm going to Delhi, to my own home, to Shyam,' she said loudly, causing the forever-married lady to take a couple of steps back.

Rustom was whining now. 'But you can't do that! What about all my plans? Please Mini, my future depends on it!'

Mini disconnected. She was puzzled. Did Rustom envisage a future with her? Could it be that he really cared? Maybe she had it all wrong. Maybe Rustom would actually divorce Wheelchair and marry her?

The line shuffled forward. Mini moved, still confused. Her

phone rang again. It was Shyam. 'Hi Shyam, I am in the queue for check in, so I'll see you in a few hours, I guess,' she said.

'That's great!' Shyam said, sounding tired. 'Take a prepaid cab, alright? I would have picked you up, but I can't leave Polka alone,' he continued. Mini's ears pricked as a female voice purred in the background.

'You go ahead Shyam, I'll keep an eye on things here,' it said.

Mini's antennae rose in suspicion. 'Shyam, who's that with you?'

'Oh, it's just Muffin's mom,' Shyam said dismissively.

Mini was aghast. Who was Muffin's mom? she wondered. Was she behind Shyam's divorce threat? She would find out soon enough, Mini thought dourly.

Her phone rang again. It was Rustom, drunk as a skunk, she could tell. 'Mini, please come. My heart is breaking. I'm going to kill myself. I can see the waves from my window, Mini. They are calling me,' he slurred into the phone.

Mini got worried. Would Rustom really jump into the sea? 'Rustom! You're drunk! Don't do anything foolish,' she spoke urgently.

Rustom was undeterred. 'It's all over. She's leaving … on a jet plane, dunno when she'll be back again…'

'You're crazy, man! Go to sleep!' she hissed into the phone.

'I can't do anything without you. I need you so much, I don't know what to do,' Rustom whined.

Alarm bells jolted Mini's conscience. She had never heard Rustom talk like this. She panicked. What if he really killed himself? She saw a horrid vision of herself in jail, locked up for abetting suicide. She couldn't have Rustom dying because of her. She would have to go to Goa, sort Rustom out and catch a later flight home.

Mini picked up her bags and shifted to the Goa check-in queue.

The phone buzzed again. 'Sicko' was flashing on the screen again. Mini's fingers clenched around the phone. She didn't answer it. Instead she sent a brief text message. 'Work crisis. Have to make an urgent detour to Goa, will take later flight.'

It was a particularly turbulent flight. But Mini's inner turbulence rendered her immune. She wondered what she would encounter at Rustom's den. She would have to get him sobered down and make sure he wasn't suicidal. And then, she would go home and find out who Muffin's mom was. It served her right, Mini thought woefully. She had thought she could have her cake and eat it too, keep her husband *and* a dream lover. Now, it seemed, she had lost both. Silent tears trickled down her eyes. The stress was catching up. All this relationship stuff was hard work, she thought bitterly. Why was her happiness so dependent on men? Why couldn't she love 'em-leave 'em? Why couldn't she like women instead? Why couldn't she be like the forever-married lady? All she had wanted was a memorable pause before menopause. Was she really asking for too much?

Mini's fear of flying kicked in belatedly as the plane started its descent with a thump. She clutched the sides of her seat and scrunched her eyes shut, waiting to die. A mad thought occurred to her. If the plane crashed into the ocean and Rustom jumped into the sea, maybe they would unite in the water. But the plane landed without mishap and taxied to a halt, spilling Mini out into the balmy, sea-laden air of Goa.

At the airport, everyone seemed to be in the holiday mood. But Mini's heart was full of foreboding. What was she going to find, she wondered. A quick trip to the loo was in order. Mini touched up her lipstick, changed into a flattering blouse and sprayed some perfume. She rummaged in her bags for her high-heeled shoes and slipped them on. As she brushed her hair and sucked in her stomach, she told herself that she wasn't dressing up for Rustom. It was just war paint, ammunition for the mission, she reasoned. There wasn't a moment to delay, the crazy, drunken man might be already heading into the water, she thought, pausing before a shop window to check out her reflection.

Rustom had enclosed directions to his place along with the ticket. Mini hopped into a taxi and sped away into the dusk. Goa was the setting for many of her romantic fantasies with Rustom, but right then, all she wanted was to find Rustom and make sure he was safe. She would check on him and take the night flight to Delhi. From one stupid man to another, she thought moodily.

The sun was setting and the sea was a picture of tranquility. Only Mini's mind was in turmoil. Many years ago, Shyam had threatened to jump off a train and she had ended up marrying him. Now Rustom was doing the same thing. Her karma was following her.

Mini didn't want to deal with a drunken, suicidal Rustom. And she certainly didn't want to face Shyam's condemnation. She wished she could hug Polka and sleep for a few days.

★ ★ ★

Rustom poured himself another stiff one, all set to get rip-roaring drunk. He had been so excited about Mini coming over. They would have finally got some time together, without worrying about wagging tongues and prying eyes. He would have unfolded all his plans for the two of them and watched her face light up like a child's. Besides, it had taken weeks to persuade Nilufer's flint stone of a dad to put money in the new venture. He was going to blow his top when he found out that Mini had backed out.

He had gone to so much trouble too, Rustom thought bitterly. Gomes had put candles everywhere. The old dining table had been dusted and dragged out to the beach, its permanent food stains covered with a tablecloth. The stars were out in full force. The wine was on ice. He had even tuned his old guitar and strewn fragrant flowers on the bed. The partnership papers were ready, awaiting signature. Had Gomes hired a horse instead of a donkey, he would have even done a swayamvar on Mini. And suddenly, Mini wanted to go back to her husband?

Why didn't she get it? They were so right for each other, in every way. Now his dreams for them were about to go down the drain, he thought. Mini had pulled the rug from beneath his feet. Women were deceitful. He should never have trusted her.

* * *

Shyam read Mini's text message and came to an instant decision. This sudden detour to Goa was rather suspicious. He was going after Mini and bringing her home. This time, either she came away with him or it was all over.

The Parsi had something to do with this sudden change of plans, he could bet on it, Shyam thought. A quick call to the detective confirmed his suspicions. Not for a minute did Shyam blame Mini. It was the Parsi who had led her on. Mini was too naive to engineer anything so devious. He had to save her. Shyam requested Muffin's mom to take care of Polka and took the next flight to Goa.

It looked more like a zoo than a den, Mini thought, as the taxi slid to a halt outside a broken gate. A donkey was grazing in the sparse grass beyond the outer fence. A couple of stray dogs loitered about. She could hear the sea waves murmuring in the distance. Hopefully, Rustom was not floating on them.

She wheeled her suitcase down the overgrown garden trail. It proved to be treacherous path, as first her heel and then, a moment later, her suitcase wheel got stuck in the mud and came off. With great difficulty, Mini dragged herself to the dimly-lit porch. She was about to ring the doorbell when her foot encountered something soft and furry. It was a stray pup, a skinny little bedraggled waif, curled up on the doormat, shivering silently. Mini's heart melted. She scooped him up and put him on one side, out of harm's way. Removing the stole she had around her shoulders, she folded it and draped it over his frail body. Poor little thing, Mini thought. She must get Rustom to feed him some warm milk.

She pressed the doorbell. There was no response. Had Rustom jumped off already? Mini pushed the door open and found him right in front of her.

He was sitting all alone in a room bathed in the soft glow of candles. White curtains fluttered in the breeze. Empty bottles and a wine glass stood on the table before him.

Rustom looked up. It was Mini.

She had come. Now he would never let her go. He had won.

He got up on unsteady feet and pulled her into his arms. 'Hi there. So I wasn't dreaming, it is you,' he murmured into her ear.

'Came to see if you are alright,' Mini replied defensively, turning away her face from the sour smell of wine on his breath.

'As long as you're here...' Rustom replied, holding her tight.

Mini pulled away, upset with Rustom. There was nothing wrong with him. He wasn't dead or crazed and on the verge of suicide. 'I wish I hadn't!' she said. 'You are not dying or anything.'

Rustom grinned. This was what he loved about this woman. She was original.

'I'm leaving, taking the next flight to Delhi,' Mini said.

Rustom tightened his embrace. 'Stay a while. Please,' he pleaded. Mini wriggled, trying to get away.

Rustom's nearness was playing havoc with her resolve. 'Oh no, the husband's waiting,' she replied.

'Then why did you come?' Rustom asked artfully.

'Because you were threatening to kill yourself?' Mini replied, managing to put some distance between them.

'Come here,' Rustom ordered, reaching out for Mini again.

Mini stood uncertainly, paralyzed by indecision. 'I have to go home. Don't want to miss the last flight,' she said breathlessly, her heart doing somersaults.

'Please, at least stay for dinner,' Rustom pleaded.

'Dinner. That's all,' Mini relented.

'Yes, dinner, that's all,' agreed Rustom, with a sloppy smile.

Rustom had been making careful preparations. The stage had been set for seduction. The sea waves would make music and the candlelight would give everything an air of romance, he hoped. Except for the donkey, everything was perfect.

Mini sat down, still looking tentative. Rustom poured wine into glasses and lifted his glass to raise a toast. 'To us,' he said, leaning forward.

Mini gulped down the wine like it was a life-saving drug. She would have a drink or two and go back to the airport, she decided. 'I need to use the loo,' she said.

Rustom led her inside. Mini went into a bedroom and quickly called the airline. 'Put me on the night flight to Delhi please,' she requested.

She was put on hold for the longest time before the airline

official came back on the line. 'I am sorry, Ma'am. The last flight has been cancelled due to bad weather. Can I put you on the first flight out in the morning?'

Mini was too shocked to reply. The possibility of a flight cancellation hadn't occurred to her. She would have to call Shyam right away. But what was she going to tell him? And what was she to tell Rustom?

Her phone's battery was dying. Mini opened her suitcase to pull out her mobile charger when something red fell out. It was her naughty red negligeé. A crystal clear sign. Mini picked up it up and ran herself a scented bath.

Rustom cursed himself for drinking too much wine. It was making him sleepy and sluggish. He wanted everything to be perfect for Mini. Quickly, he gargled, splashed water on his face and picked up his guitar. When Mini emerged from the washroom, she would find him singing, poised on bended knee. Which woman could resist a serenade, Rustom thought with an inebriated smile.

He looked up and saw a gorgeous vision in diaphanous red, swaying towards him. It was Mini, looking sexy as hell. What was that she was wearing or not wearing, he wondered, his pulse racing.

Mini drifted slowly across the verandah, feeling like the heroine from one of her favourite romances. Rustom finished his serenade and switched on the stereo. A husky Latino voice came on. He held out his arms and they danced, bodies welded together. The sensuous music added to the enchantment.

Rustom was flawless, Mini thought, gazing at him, shivering with anticipation. Feeling her quiver, he silently draped his coat around her. Mini flew to cloud nine. Her heart thudded and her stomach tied itself in knots. She had chosen to stay. She had very consciously decided to debut her red negligeé. Rustom was going to confess his love for her. And when two people were in love, nothing could stand in the way. Tomorrow, they would worry about Wheelchair. And about Shyam. Tonight there would be only confessions, admissions and declarations.

# 8

---

A dreamy-eyed Mini allowed Rustom to lead her inside. He opened the door to his bedroom. Soft lamplight threw languid shadows on the bed. Mini's skin was awash with delicious sensations as she felt silken sheets beneath her. Rose petals were strewn all over the room. A scented candle diffused a musky scent. Mini's romantic fantasies had come alive.

Pushing her back against the pillows, Rustom stroked her cheek with one finger. 'What comes after the wedding?' he asked. Mini gazed into his eyes questioningly.

'The honeymoon,' he whispered huskily into her ear.

Of course, thought Mini. The great, royal wedding was over and she was about to take off on her second honeymoon. Tonight was going to be a buffet, Mini decided as she felt Rustom nibbling at the tender skin on her throat. She was going to sample everything on the menu. For appetizers, she would try aching, long and lingering foreplay; nice and slow, with every lick and bite savoured. Followed by a main course so varied and experimental, it would defy imagination. And then, some utterly sinful, delectable dessert.

Mini grew impatient. The main course was taking too long

in getting ready. At this rate, it was never coming, Mini thought. It was time to take matters in hand.

Diving down, she felt between Rustom's legs. He was limp.

'This never happens, Mini,' Rustom huffed. 'I think I drank too much wine,' he said lamely, as he flopped back on the pillows and, to her utter disbelief, fell asleep.

Mini felt like a truck had run over her fantasies.

Rustom had failed to rise to her expectations. Even worse, he was sleeping with his mouth open and was snoring, like a hog.

Her Dream Lover snored?

Mini wanted to throw up. She couldn't bear to spend another moment around him. She had to get away, it didn't matter where. She grabbed some paper lying on the bedside table, wanting to scribble a scathing note before disappearing.

What was her name doing on it? Mini sat down to read.

Things were going from bad to worse. Rustom had drawn a full partnership agreement with her, for a start-up wedding planning agency. His signatures were already in place. Obviously, she was expected to add hers.

Mini didn't remember giving him a go ahead, not in so many words. They hadn't even discussed the matter in detail. Did he think she would fall in with his plans so easily? Talk about being taken for granted, she thought, furious with Rustom. Men needed to be put in their place. Rustom couldn't even get it up but expected her to prop up his future. Shyam needed her to fulfill his domestic needs but he didn't care two hoots about what she needed.

She could do without either of them. They were the ones who needed her. From now on, she would take care of herself, no need for unnecessary appendages. She would be alone, like

Lily Malone. It would be tough but it was do-able, Mini thought. After all, thousands of women survived on their own, like Aditi. And Shailaja Kumari.

She was just dragging her suitcase out of the hall when Rustom woke up.

'Where are you going Mini?' he asked plaintively.

'I'm leaving. And I won't be coming back,' she replied tersely.

'But...but what about us? Our future together?' Rustom blurted.

'What future? Don't make me laugh, Rustom,' Mini replied.

'You know I can't leave my wife, she is an invalid and she needs me,' he whined, trailing behind her, looking helpless.

Pathetic, thought Mini. Had she actually seen perfection in this sorry specimen of manhood? 'Sure, stay with your wife,' she said, with a careless laugh. 'Don't worry about us. So we slept together a few times, big deal. What did you think, I'm in love with you?' Mini said, cursing her wobbly suitcase and broken sandal, impediments to a speedy getaway.

Rustom walked faster, intent on stopping her. As Mini stepped out from the front door, the little stray pup ran towards her, wagging his tail with all his might. But before Mini could pick him up, Rustom kicked him hard in the ribs. The puppy yelped in pain and flew across the path. He lay there, whimpering piteously, his cries echoing in the dark.

Mini saw red. Picking up the injured pup, she delivered her parting shot. 'I could never love a man who can't love a dog. It's over, Rustom. Frankly, I never had any feelings for you. You are just a good lay, Rustom. Or should I say, were?'

Rustom's pleading voice followed her as she marched on. 'Please Mini, don't go. Did I do something wrong?' he snivelled.

Mini didn't even look back. Head held high, she walked out of Rustom's life, slamming the door on him.

* * *

It was raining. Handicapped by her suitcase and sandal, Mini made scant progress. But anything was better than spending the night with Rustom, Mini was certain. What kind of man kicked a puppy? Had Shyam been there, he would have kicked Rustom where it hurts. How could she have been so blind? Did he really expect her to sign that agreement? Did he think she was a pushover? Carefully, Mini put the puppy on the ground. He howled pitifully, peed and curled up against her suitcase.

Alone, Mini waited for a taxi to pass by. After half an hour, she figured that there weren't any. The rain hadn't stopped either. It was pitch dark. She shivered with cold and misgiving. Her phone had run out of battery. What on earth had she landed herself in, Mini thought, cursing Rustom.

There wasn't a soul in sight. Even the puppy abandoned her to take shelter in a ditch. What was she going to do? Nobody except Shyam and Rustom knew that she was in Goa. There was no chance of a rescue.

The ringing of distant church bells announced the passage of another hour. The sky was dark with clouds and foreboding. Mini started to get frightened. Her eyes were burning and she sneezed for the hundredth time. On top of that, she'd barely eaten anything since the morning, her stomach reminded her with a growl. She could kill for a mug of steaming hot soup. Plus she urgently needed to go to the bathroom. Maybe this was the end, thought Mini. She was going to die of pneumonia. How would Polka go through life without her? And Shyam? Slumped against the suitcase, a miserable Mini fell into an uncomfortable doze.

After what seemed like an eternity, a taxi screeched to a halt next to her. A hand dragged her into the cab. Mini's worst fears were coming true. She was going to be kidnapped and murdered by the Goa mafia.

'Mini! Thank god!' a familiar voice exclaimed. It was Shyam.

She fell into his arms and sobbed into his shoulder, hugging him like she would never let go.

★ ★ ★

Shyam had booked himself a room and a fast car at the airport. He was on his way to the Parsi's place. It was taking forever to reach there. Would he find Mini? Would eighteen years of togetherness come to nought? Was the marriage over? He was sick with apprehension.

He peered out of the window. The sea looked stormy. The road was dark and slick with rain, with trees casting sinister shadows. Nobody in their right minds would be out in this crazy, turbulent night.

The car headlights shone on something bright pink. It was a suitcase. Could it be...? But who else on earth had a hot pink suitcase? He asked the driver to stop the car.

It was her. Soaking wet, woebegone, lost, holding on to her bright pink suitcase like a lifeline.

Quickly, he bundled her up into the cab and sped away to his hotel. Whatever make-up she had worn had washed off, leaving her bare and vulnerable. Her forehead felt hot to touch and her teeth were chattering. She had obviously caught a bad chill, the poor thing, Shyam thought, a rush of protective feelings swamping him.

'What happened, Mini? Hmm? Where were you going?' he asked, his voice full of concern.

'I was coming home,' she replied as she hugged his neck and burst into a fresh flood of tears.

Shyam's heart melted into a puddle of tender emotions. His Mini had chosen to come back home to him. Nothing else mattered. The questions and recriminations could wait. Whatever had happened with the Parsi was over. He'd got Mini back and this time, it was for keeps.

Maybe Mini had actually come to Goa to handle a work crisis. Maybe the Parsi was just a colleague. The work must have finished and Mini must have been on her way home. That mad Parsi could have at least found his wife a cab, Shyam thought, a wave of anger sweeping through him as he held Mini close.

A silent, subdued Mini trailed Shyam into his hotel room. Shyam ran a steaming bath and gently placed Mini in it. Then he called room service for chicken soup. When he peeped into the bathroom a little later, he found her fast asleep in the bath tub. He lifted her to the bed and tucked her into the covers.

Mini tried to speak. 'I'm sorry...' she said, her eyes droopy with sleep.

Shyam shushed her as he spooned hot soup into her mouth. 'Go to sleep, Baby. It's late and we have an early flight home,' he said, gently kissing her forehead as he rocked her in his arms.

Home. Such a beautiful word, Mini thought, treasuring the feelings the word evoked as she drifted off into a dreamless sleep.

When she opened her eyes, she found Shyam next to her. Was he mad at her, she wondered. But what she saw in his face set her pulse racing. She was wearing his kurta and it had ridden up her thighs. Shyam pushed it up till it bunched about her neck and made achingly gentle love to her.

It was like the old times, Mini exulted, before they were even married. Shyam was hungry for her again. Everything was familiar, yet every sensation was new. Piping hot kaali daal topped with fresh, homemade, white butter, Mini thought, awash with pleasure. Luscious seekh kebabs, textured on the outside, silken on the inside, melting in the mouth, an explosion of sweet déjà vu. It had been so long, far too long since they had come together, Mini thought, tears of regret mixed with relief sliding down her cheeks. With Shyam, there was no pressure to look her best, all the time. She didn't have to hide her stretch marks or suck in her paunch, Mini thought happily.

On the flight back home, Shyam held Mini's hand throughout, not letting go even when breakfast was served. Single-handedly, he demolished his food tray, made short work of hers and asked the amused flight attendant for another helping. Mini smiled to herself. That was Shyam for you, she thought, unapologetic, in-your-face, honest. And he was all hers.

★ ★ ★

The familiar roads of South Delhi were like balm for Mini. As the cab entered her colony, she drank in the cool breeze laden with the scents of Mogra and Madhumalti. The Gulmohar and Amaltas were in full bloom, the dappled sunshine sweet on her skin. After grimy Mumbai, Delhi was like paradise regained.

Mini took one look at the house and got into action. She dusted, mopped, scrubbed and polished. She arranged flowers in vases. She reclaimed the kitchen and cooked matar-aloo for Shyam. A little later, when Mini was making dessert, Polka served up a delightful surprise. Twelve skinny pups, scrambling blindly, falling and tumbling over each other to get milk. It was a sight worth coming home for.

As the days melted into each other, Mini felt a warm glow inside. After the emotional roller coaster she had been on, familiarity was so comforting. There was a great satisfaction in caring for her home and husband. In making the morning tea, cooking omelettes, weeding the garden. Her world was normal. She was back in stride and it felt good.

She went back to the Soul Mates Delhi office, slipping comfortably into her old routine. At home, she watched her grandpups grow. They rolled, tumbled and ran away with Mini's slippers. A matronly Polka kept a benign eye on them, occasionally intervening to rebuke a particularly boisterous one who bullied his weaker brethren. Shyam gifted the pick of the litter to Muffin's mom. Mini felt a flash of jealousy but hid it behind a smile. It was too early to rock the boat again.

Every now and then, Rustom would pop up in her mind like a bad dream. He had gone ahead and formed his own company, taking away several Mumbai clients of Soul Mates. He had also poached Sandra.  Apparently, he had partnered with Benaifer Reporter, the creative head of Parsi Matrimony. Mini felt mildly cheated. The man had sworn allegiance to her. But maybe, just maybe, Rustom hadn't failed her; maybe she was the one who had failed Rustom. She wanted him to be perfect, like the heroes in her romance novels – permanently sporting a sexy stubble, an enticing drawl and a hard-on. Who could live up to that?

All men farted, crapped, snorted, smelt and burped. No relationship could stay romantic beyond courtship. Once the sexual attraction faded, domesticity and complacency crept in. Life was like that, Shyam wasn't to blame.

Aditi sent her a bunch of Sufi CDs. Mini got a terrible shock when she read the descriptions on the CD covers. She had mistaken prayers for love ditties. The music was about spiritual, not sexual gratification. Maybe that was where her salvation lay. She would atone for her sins by becoming a closet Sufi. Goodbye Greek gods, hello god.

She tried to get Shyam into spirituality but he declared that Tendulkar was the only god he knew.

Dhira called from Mumbai, nursing a broken heart. She had met her Mr Right and was ready to leave her husband for him. But Mr Right refused to marry her. Dhira told Mini that she would wait till Mr Right was ready.

Mini gave her sage advice. 'A bird in hand is better than two in the bush.'

She herself had held on to Shyam. It didn't matter that she did not love him the way that she had before. And yes, he was rather clumsy when it came to expressing affection. But he was there for her when she needed him most. That, Mini had realized, counted for a lot.

The ordinary and constant is always essential in life, much like the sun's cyclical journey around the world. Mini's quest had come a full circle.

The second coming she had awaited was a homecoming.

# Acknowledgements

A first book of a lazy person owes gratitude to almost everyone in the universe, including the universe. To begin with, I need to thank Kavita Bhanot, who inspired me to change a half-written screenplay into this novel. Hopefully, the screenplay will get written by and by.

Next, I must thank that snobby cafe at the Jaipur Literature Festival where a chance meeting with Hoshang Merchant led me to the gracious Karthika and the rest, as they say, is history.

Other than that, everyone at HarperCollins India, especially Karthika who I cannot thank enough, Shantanu, Ramona, Neelini, Bonita and Rashi; the folks at Ogilvy, including Piyush Pandey for his generosity, Preeti Koul Chaudhry for putting her heart into creating the cover design and Ajay Gahlaut for his unstinted encouragement over endless cups of coffee; various Club Mahindra resorts and Writers Hill for allowing me some peace and quiet for writing; Dr Alok Sarin for being my entire rainbow coalition; www.cookingwithsomehelp.wordpress.com for cheering me on, all along; Shekhar, Karuna and Sweta for their prayers and endless enquiries of 'Finished?' so that I was left with no choice but to do so.

# BETRAYED

## KAVITA DASWANI

*How far should a girl go to get what she wants?*

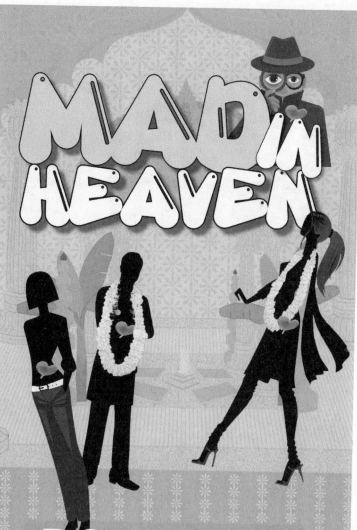

# MAD IN HEAVEN

## P.G. Bhaskar

# FAHAD SAMAR

# flash point

## Lust, fraud & naked ambition

# I DO!
## Do I?

# RUCHITA
# MISRA

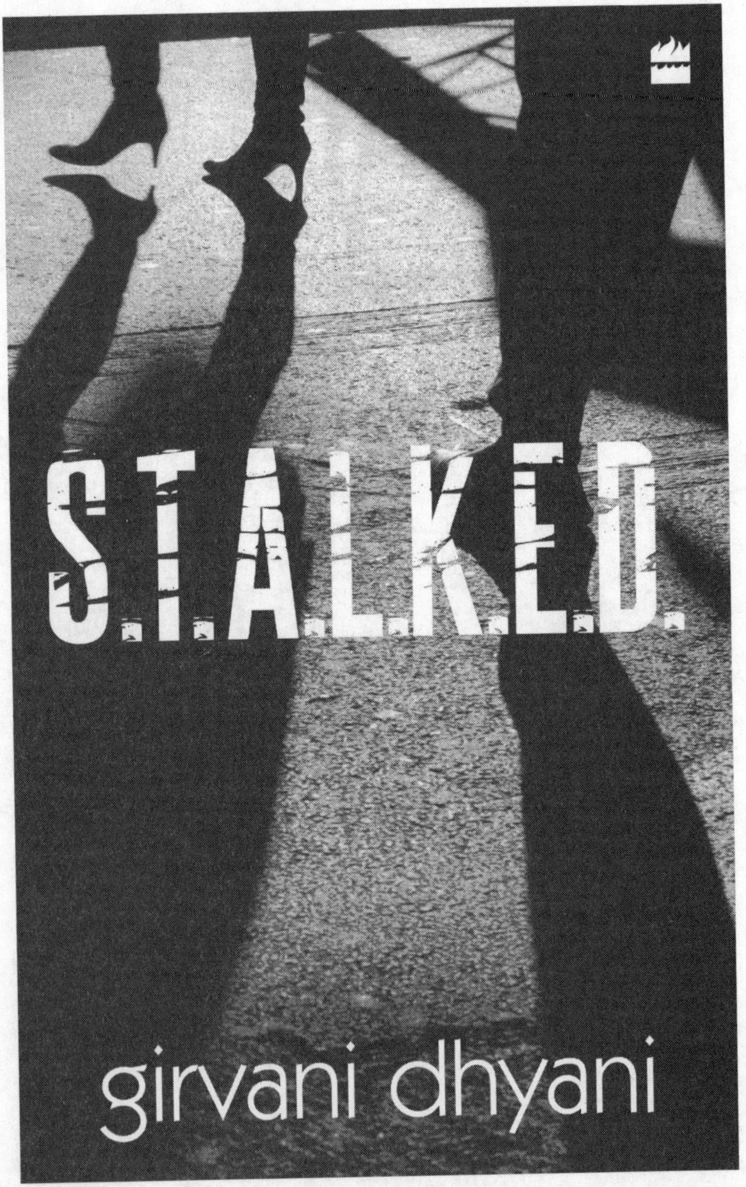
S.T.A.L.K.E.D.
girvani dhyani